THE CURSE OF WARNER MANOR

The Farrington Phenomenon 1

Lovelyn Bettison

contents

Prologue

My breath ragged, I stared into the darkness with my heart hammering in my chest. I had been plagued by nightmares ever since I could remember. I rarely made it through the night without waking at least once with a tightness in my chest and the feeling that I was being watched. I never remembered the nightmares when I woke. I only felt the pressing dread that lingered after them.

I sat up and switched on the bedside lamp. Soft, yellow light spilled into the darkness. My room was empty, as it should have been, but something wasn't right. Nothing in my life had ever felt right.

I could hear voices outside—a couple arguing in the dead of night. I listened to their angry words and took slow, intentional breaths to calm my pounding heart.

I had learned to stuff down my anxiety. It was nothing. They were normal. Everyone felt anxiety when they were about to embark on a new business venture. I had just made the biggest purchase of my career and was ready to begin renovations on a house that belonged to one of my favorite artists. It was natural to be nervous. That's what

I told myself as I switched off the light and tried to go back to sleep. Worry and self-doubt spinning in my head, I closed my eyes and hoped no more nightmares would come. I needed to sleep.

In the morning, I would pack and ignore the sinking feeling in my chest. What was done was done. I'd made commitments. I'd signed all the paperwork and started the wheels in motion. Now I had a project to finish. I'd put on a happy face and find the excitement in it. After all, it was a dream come true, wasn't it?

CHAPTER 1

I stood in the horseshoe driveway, looking up at the house. Normally, I would never buy a place without first visiting it in person, but this one was special. I knew it the day the auction flyer showed up in my mailbox. I recognized the house immediately and had to have it.

Warner Manor had a rich history. It had passed through many hands but none as famous as Raoul Bonnaire. He had taken the art world by storm in the seventies and bought the manor at the height of his success.

It was a piece of history. I'd only seen pictures of the place in the popular magazines of the time. After Raoul's death, the manor was held in trust. Unfortunately, the trust left it to rot for years before one day mysteriously deciding to put it up for auction. I'd assumed I would have to fight off many competitors flush with cash to win the auction. I was wrong. Strangely, no one else was interested.

Using my hand to block the sun, I looked up at the massive home. It was a sight to behold, even in its shabby, run-down state. Emerald-green vines climbed the brick façade, stretching over windows and reaching the roof. I could already see places where pebble-sized chunks of mortar had crumbled, leaving small piles of rubble around the foundation. Still, the building was grand. The original house was constructed in 1752. Over the years, more and more had been added, turning it into the mansion it had become. Most would assume it would need to be demolished, but I could never let that happen. Restoring Warner Manor to its former glory would take hundreds of thousands of dollars. I knew that before ever stepping inside, but this house was special.

I heard the crush of gravel beneath tires and turned to see a silver Mercedes creeping into the driveway. It parked behind my car. Alton Richardson, my realtor, got out. He was a tall mahogany-colored man in a light gray suit and black dress shoes polished to perfection. Uniform black waves cascaded across his scalp. When he saw me, he smiled, revealing straight, perfectly white teeth. "Khadijah." He buttoned his suit jacket with one hand as he walked toward me. In the other hand, he held a bottle of champagne decorated with a red ribbon. "How do you feel now that it's finally yours?" Noticing that I was looking at the bottle in his hand, he extended it to me. "To christen the new house." He smiled, revealing the dimple on his left cheek.

"Thank you." I took the bottle from him. Seeing him in his suit and his shiny shoes suddenly made me feel self-conscious about my ratty T-shirt and jeans. I hadn't even bothered to put on makeup that morning. Without a little bit of contouring, my cheeks were as full and round as a chipmunk's. My hair was slicked back into a low nub of a ponytail. I found myself wishing I'd at least put on a little bit of lip gloss and some earrings, but I knew coming to a place that had been abandoned for so long in anything fancier than jeans and a T-shirt would have been a mistake. I wasn't there to work on the first day, but I needed to get a good look at the place to know what we'd be working with. "Do you want to take a look around with me?" Of course, I was interested in keeping him around for as long as possible. I could never tire of watching him, and even though the manor was mine now, I didn't want to explore it alone. Anything could be lurking inside. I was courageous, but I wasn't stupid. I knew that poking around in a long-abandoned building alone was risky, and having a bit of company would calm the anxiety I was still feeling about my purchase.

Alton looked back toward his car, and I was sure he would say no, but he surprised me. "Sure. I've got a few minutes before my next appointment."

With Alton at my side, I unlocked the front door. It creaked on its hinges and swung open, revealing what had at one time been the grandest of entryways. Twin staircases arched toward the second floor on both sides of the foyer. Their banisters, splintered and broken, lay in pieces on the floor. An elaborate chandelier hung precariously from the ceiling by one wire. Even in this dilapidated condition, I could imagine what this house must've been like before it had been left to decay. I could picture myself entering the foyer and being greeted by the frenetic sounds of jazz playing beneath the chatter of a spirited conversation in the next room. The image was so clear it could've been real. I wished it had been. I longed to know what had happened here when Raoul was still living.

No music greeted us. Only musty air wafted out at us, letting me know there was probably water damage somewhere in the house. Alton looked at me, crinkling his nose before gesturing to the doorway.

"After you," he said.

I stepped inside. It was a broken shell of what it once was. Glimpses of its historic past caught my eye everywhere I looked. Ornately carved wooden roses embellished the broken banisters. Such a shame. I already knew I would try to get them restored. Wiping the dust on the floor away with the toe of my sneaker revealed finely veined black marble beneath our feet. I could imagine the care that went into building this home. As I took in the initial sights, I noticed a massive canvas lying upside down in the middle of the staircase to the left. I set the champagne bottle on the floor next to the door and immediately went to it.

"Careful." Alton walked through the door as I cautiously stepped up onto the first stair. It creaked but seemed firm beneath my feet.

Gingerly, I climbed to the center of the staircase. I knew the odds were slim, but I hoped it would be a Raoul original. I picked it up, letting the debris slide off before turning it over and getting a look at it. It wasn't one of Raoul's. Of course not. Something that valuable wouldn't have lasted overturned on the staircase for this long. Still, I had been hopeful. Though it wasn't one of Raoul's, there was still something about the painting I liked. It was a picture of the house painted in an Impressionist style, as if the artist was lying in the grass a distance away. Muted lavender and yellow flowers dotted the foreground. The manor rose out of the field like a fortress.

"Is it one of his?" Alton stood by the front door, craning his neck to see the painting from where he stood.

I turned to him, careful not to lose my footing. "No, but I like it." I stepped to the side slightly and held the painting up so he could see it.

"Yeah, it's nice." The way he averted his eyes made me think he was lying, but it didn't matter if he liked it. I did. When the renovation was over, I would find a place for it. I leaned the painting against the wall and looked up the stairs. Garbage littered the staircase: old Coca-Cola bottles, a worn-out sneaker, a dented can of chili, bits of plaster and broken wood, dangerously placed screws and nails, and too many other things to list. Since I was already halfway up the stairs, I decided to explore the second floor first. "Are you ready to look around?" I asked as I continued up the steps. The wooden staircase groaned.

Alton clapped his hands together. "I'll wait until you get all the way up. I don't trust this thing can hold both of us at once."

"You can use that one." I pointed to the twin staircase opposite me. As I did, I noticed the split in the side of the structure.

Alton looked at it for a moment before returning his gaze to me. Arching an eyebrow, he said, "I'll take my chances with this one."

"I don't blame you." I climbed tentatively to the second floor, noticing how the stairs creaked with each step.

The smell of dampness was more pungent on the second floor. It tucked itself uncomfortably inside my nostrils. I imagined the worst: black mold. That would be a nightmare to correct, but I couldn't pretend I didn't expect it.

The hallway was more expansive than most. Two of me could stand in the center with arms outstretched and still not touch either wall. Though the hallway was wide, somehow, it still felt confined.

"It has so much potential. Too bad they let it rot for so long." He walked ahead of me up the hallway and pushed the first door open. It squeaked on its hinges, revealing a spacious room. Brightly colored potato chip bags littered the floor. A dirty mattress lay in the corner, a brown stain the shape of Texas in the center.

"Squatters?" My heart clenched. Maybe we weren't alone.

Alton shook his head. "This room has been like this for a while." He strode in and kicked the dirty mattress with his shiny black shoe. "There were squatters in here a while back, but they were all cleared out before it ever went up for auction."

I swallowed a lump in my throat. "I hope you're right."

"You're a pro at this. Don't let a few squatters scare you." He turned around to face me as I stood in the doorway, and his mouth dropped open.

"What?" I asked.

"That's new." He looked at the wall next to the door, so I walked inside, turning to see what had caught his attention.

"What is that?" Rough red lines marked the wall. Curves and straight lines all came together to form the crude drawing of a man with a chaotic scribble of circles where his head should have been. Eight pentagrams surrounded the figure as if trapping it. It isn't uncommon to find graffiti on the walls of houses that have been abandoned for as long as this one, but this graffiti was different from the usual gang tags or declarations of love. Something about the image unsettled me. My stomach dropped, and my chest fluttered with fear. I reached up to touch the pedant I usually wore around my neck. It was a habit. I often fiddled with it when nervous, but it wasn't hanging below my collarbone. I'd momentarily forgotten I'd lost it before leaving on this trip. My life had been such a whirlwind recently that I'd misplaced many things: my wallet on multiple occasions, my keys, my favorite pair of shoes.

"I don't know," Alton walked forward, so he stood next to me, "but it is interesting. Maybe you could sell it." He chuckled and shoved his hands into his pockets before rocking forward onto the balls of his feet.

"I'm sure it's worth millions." I shook my head and turned away from it.

"Maybe you should have someone bless this place, just in case. My grandmother could—"

"Bless this place?" I couldn't believe what he was saying.

"You know, with all the stuff that happened here—" He gestured to the wall with an open palm.

"What do you mean?" I narrowed my eyes at him.

His expression fell. "I assumed you knew. I mean, you said you're an expert on Raoul."

I had indeed spent my life studying his work. It spoke to me in a way no art ever had. The bold lines and vibrant colors of his painting called out to me. His work was so full of joy, but toward the end of his life, Raoul fell into darkness. "You mean the rituals?"

"Yeah." He looked back at me. "I think that's why no one did anything with it for so long. Everybody was afraid to touch it, including the trust in charge of the property. They probably only decided to dump it at auction because they didn't think they could sell it any other way."

"Seriously?" I tried my best to hide the trepidation I felt ever since I bought the manor. I'd convinced myself those feelings were rooted in the enormous expense I was taking on and nothing else.

He threw his head back as if in disbelief. "So, you're too sophisticated to be afraid of that kind of thing?"

I shook my head. "I didn't say anything about being sophisticated, but I'm not superstitious." A great crash rumbled through the house, and I nearly jumped out of my skin. We looked at each other before hurrying down the hallway to the stairs to find the source of the noise.

"That was close." Davida stood by the front door, looking up at us. The entryway chandelier lay broken at her feet.

"Thank God you're okay." I rushed down the stairs, momentarily forgetting they could tumble to the ground, much like the chandelier.

Davida and I started working together during my third house flip. I found her after a contractor I'd worked with majorly screwed me over. That ordeal halved my profits. What a fiasco! I learned a lot from the whole experience though, and I met Davida because of it. I found her on a forum when I was looking for someone new to work with, and we'd been partnering up ever since.

Davida was a round-faced woman in her late forties with short graying hair. She had an approachable sophistication even in her work clothes, a flannel shirt, jeans, and construction boots. She smiled widely and hugged me. "Looks like we've got our work cut out for us." She looked down at the shattered chandelier on the floor. Before I could comment, she noticed Alton standing at the top of the stairs. "And who is this?" She raised an eyebrow.

Alton navigated the staircase more carefully than I had. "Alton Richardson. I'm the realtor."

"So, you sold Khadijah this money pit." Davida winked at me. She thought I was crazy for taking this on. She was probably right.

"The purchase was all her. I'm just here to facilitate the process." He held up his empty palms as if that would somehow absolve him of all guilt. "This place was a real steal. If you two can fix up everything that's wrong with it..." He gestured around the entryway. "You could have a massive moneymaker on your hands."

"That's why I'm here. I'm going to have this place looking better than new." Davida's enthusiasm was part of the reason I ended up working with her. That and the fact that, from our very first project, she proved that she knew how to do top-quality work and find the best prices on grade-A materials. She also had a knack for hiring good, honest workers. Before her, I struggled with that. As time went on, I realized working with her made my life easier. Eventually, she became more involved in projects until we were more like business partners.

"I'm not talking about what's physically wrong with the place." He glanced down at his watch. "I've got to get going. I have another client to see." He walked between us to the front door. "Good luck with the whole ghost, occult thing," he said over his shoulder before stepping outside.

Davida waited until his footsteps faded before she spoke. "What was that about?" She stepped around the broken chandelier further into the house.

I shook my head. "Just superstitious nonsense."

"Don't tell me you bought a haunted house." Davida guffawed.

"That's what the locals say." I pulled the door closed. I didn't want anyone else sneaking in on us while we explored the rest of the house.

"Okay. This should be interesting." Davida strolled between the two staircases into the main portion of the house.

I followed her. I'd seen the home in pictures, but being here in person was so much different. The dark marble floor stretched into the living room. Vaulted ceilings and a massive wall of windows greeted us. They looked out onto what was once a beautiful English-style garden. Now, it had become a mess of weeds, featuring mounds of trash.

"How many dumpsters do you think we'll fill cleaning this place up?" Davida walked right over to the windows and looked out into the yard.

"I'm not even going to try to guess." Pieces of a sectional couch were scattered about the room, the corner piece in front of the windows, an end piece in front of the hallway entrance. "I wish I could've been here when Raoul owned it at the height of his career. I can only imagine the parties."

Davida spun around to face me. "This is going to be the hardest project we've ever taken on, but I can't wait to see it once we're done."

Even with the dirt and graffiti, with a staircase half tumbling down and chandeliers crashing to the floor, I could see the potential in Warner Manor. I knew exactly what it could be. Davida could help me make it that. We were a team. We worked together to make things happen. I closed my eyes and could picture Warner Manor, completely renovated: walls painted, floors gleaming, this room packed full of the movers and shakers in the area. If I could pull this off, it would be the crowning achievement of my career.

****

Attics can often be the prize of any home renovation project. Sometimes, the most valuable things abandoned in an old house lay waiting in those dark cobweb-covered corners. I've made all kinds of discoveries: a wooden spinning top covered in flaking red paint that turned out to be an antique, an early nineteenth-century armoire decorated with intricate carvings, a Civil War uniform in surprisingly good condition. I even found $100,000 cash beneath the floorboards in one home.

While Davida looked around the rest of the house, getting a good idea of what it needed to make it the beauty of our dreams, curiosity drove me to the attic, anxious to see what treasures lay in wait there.

The solid cherrywood door that led to the space was closed tight. Upon seeing the keyhole, I worried that it might be locked. I turned the doorknob and pulled. Initially, the door resisted, but the rusty hinges gave way, allowing it to open stiffly. A narrow set of stairs led up to the attic.

As I ascended the old wooden staircase, I was giddy with anticipation about what I might find. Raoul could've left all manner of treasures in the house, and I was certain that, despite all the years it had been abandoned, not all of it had been looted. There must have been some very special things hidden in a dingy, neglected corner. That was why I was destined to buy this house. I'd dreamt about Raoul before that flyer ever appeared on my doorstep. Then, by what felt like a fluke,

I got the house for exactly the price I was willing to pay—a price that I knew was a long shot.

The stairs made a sharp turn toward the top, so I couldn't see into the attic before rounding the bend. I pulled the small flashlight from my pocket and shined it around the space. Piles of objects sat pushed against the walls, covered in sheets that at one time might've been white but had gone gray over the years of accumulating dust. I smiled at the mess. This was a jackpot. How could there not be something valuable here? I hoped for something beautiful of Raoul's that I could keep in my own home.

Five large boxes sat on the left side of the room next to a small teardrop-shaped window. Sunlight couldn't penetrate the grimy glass. I went over to it and tried to look out, but the dirt was too thick. I would make sure to clean it later. In the meantime, the boxes interested me. I peered inside one that was already open. It didn't seem like there was anything interesting inside at first—a few newspapers, a couple of books, and a few smaller boxes. I pulled out the newspapers. The yellowing pages were fragile to the touch. Aiming my flashlight at the page, I read it. The date at the top was June 5, 1893. I laid the paper on the floor and opened it, curious about the headlines from that year. The first article was about the low state fair attendance because of rain. The next was about an apartment block fire that killed ten people. I turned the pages carefully, mindful not to tear them, even though some bits fell apart in my hands. It was on the second page that I saw it.

A tiny square photo in the center of the second page caught my eye. A man with a sour expression looked into the camera with stern eyes. His face was familiar. I'd seen it so many times before, in magazines. on video interviews, and in my own dreams. It appeared to be a photo of Raoul Bonnaire, but Raoul was born in 1928.

The hairs on the back of my neck rose, and goosebumps formed on my arms. I crossed them over my chest, rubbing my upper arms vigorously with my hands to warm myself up.

"Are you up there?" Davida's voice floated up the stairs.

"Yeah. Come on up."

She laughed dryly. "I'd rather not."

"Don't be a scaredy-cat. You'll have to come up here eventually."

The stairs creaked under Davida's weight as she came up. Her boots were heavy on the unfinished wooden floor as she walked over to me. "I'm not a weirdo like you. I hate these old attics." She took in the surroundings before looking down to see the newspaper in my hand. "What's that?"

"Look at this." I held the paper up so she could get a good look at Raoul's picture.

She leaned over, squinting in the dim light. "What am I looking at?"

"The picture right there." I tapped the paper gently with my index finger.

She took it from me and held it close to her face.

"You really need to stop putting off getting reading glasses," I said.

"I don't need reading glasses. It's just dark in here." She held the paper away from her face. "That looks just like Raoul."

"It does, doesn't it? But look at the date on the top."

She held the paper out a little bit further. "That doesn't mean anything. He could have had this made."

She did have a point. Her explanation was a lot better than anything I had come up with. "But the paper is so fragile."

"So?" She handed it back down to me. "I'm sure they can replicate old paper."

"Back then?" I asked.

"It was the seventies, not the Stone Ages." She looked down at me.

Embarrassed, I folded the paper and put it back in the box. I would come back to it when I had some downtime to explore. "How's the rest of the house look?"

"Everything except for the staircases seems solid." She had moved to the edges of the attic and pulled her flashlight from her pocket to inspect the structure.

There was so much to get done, but I always loved this stage of a project. It was when I could most clearly see all the possibilities without the unexpected costs clouding my enthusiasm. Warner Manor was once the most spectacular home in the area, and I was going to return it to its former glory. Unfortunately, getting to that point wasn't as straightforward as I had hoped.

CHAPTER 2

W e looked through as much of the house as we could while it was still daylight. All the while, I'd hoped to find a treasure, but nothing materialized. The sun sank low in the sky as Davida and I stepped outside. We looked at the massive front garden, now completely overgrown. A sense of overwhelm passed over me. I'd taken on such a big project. I had to wrap my head around that before the work crew showed up.

As if sensing my doubt, Davida smiled at me. "It's a big job, but we'll get it done."

I exhaled, hoping to let out some of my tension. "This project is going to cost a fortune."

She chuckled. "We'll definitely go over budget. These old houses always have a lot of expensive surprises."

I shook my head. "That's what I'm afraid of."

"Don't be afraid. Embrace the challenge." She nudged me with her elbow. "Remember that brownstone we remodeled in Brooklyn?"

I laughed. "How could I forget? That was a disaster."

"When we found out that the whole place needed to be rewired, you left and just started walking up the street," she said through her laughter. "I still don't know where you thought you were going."

That seemed like a lifetime ago. I could laugh about it now, but at the time, it could've ruined me. Truth be told, it nearly did. That was so early in my career. It was surprising I decided to continue. "I don't know where I was going either. I just wanted to get away from there." I wondered what that version of me would think if she'd known that one day I'd own Warner Manor.

Sweaty and dirty, I was anxious to get back to my bed and breakfast to clean up before getting dinner. We would be here so often that making the long trip to and from the city seemed like an enormous waste of time. Anyway, I needed a break from the hustle and bustle. Some time in a quiet town upstate seemed like the perfect break. From all the pictures I'd found online, Farrington looked like the ideal place, with its sparkling lake and picturesque downtown. No wonder Raoul had decided to make it his home.

We stood in the gravel horseshoe driveway next to Davida's pickup truck. "Do you want to grab dinner?" I asked her, knowing she would probably say no.

Wiping her hands on her jeans, she looked at me with pity in her eyes. "Khadijah, you know I have to get home to the boys." I was lucky she agreed to do this job. The nearly two-hour drive was a lot. Davida had a husband and three boys: seventeen, fourteen, and twelve.

"I know. I just thought I'd ask." I looked back at the house, silhouetted against the setting sun. It gave off an air of mystery. No wonder the locals had stories about what had gone on there.

"I have to get going." Davida opened her truck door and climbed inside. "I'll be here early in the morning with the crew." She stuck her key in the ignition. "There's a lot of junk to clean out before we can do anything."

"I know." I rocked forward on my toes, stretching out the muscles in my feet. I was so tired. My body ached, and I didn't feel like I had really done much at all. "Don't waste any more time talking to me. You need to get home." I pushed the truck door closed.

The engine roared to life. Davida rolled down the window. "This place will be beautiful once it's finished."

"It sure will. Now stop talking and get going." I tapped the side of her truck with my open hand before stepping away from it. She pulled out of the driveway.

I stood in the shadow of the house with the sun dipping toward the tree line. Suddenly, I felt very alone. I pulled my keys from my pocket and walked over to the cherry-red Audi I'd rented for the trip. The gravel crunched beneath my feet, and even though I knew no one else was there, I had a distinct feeling that someone's gaze was creeping up my back. Gripping the house key between the first and second knuckle of my right hand, I spun around, prepared to jab whomever it was with it. Of course, there was no one. I scanned the darkness, looking for movement.

I took a few deep breaths, trying to calm my racing heart. Just the slightest suggestion of something sinister in the house from Alton was all it took to freak me out. I was way too suggestible. Convincing myself that I didn't see anything, I turned to go back to my car. That was when I noticed something moving in the grass in the periphery of my vision. I tightened my grip on the key and wished I had a can of pepper spray. The grass moved again, and I hurried to my car. The realization that I was out in the middle of nowhere, and it could be a wild animal in the bushes, suddenly occurred to me. I jumped into the car as quickly as possible and slammed the door. As I did, I noticed a fat raccoon waddling into the distance. I exhaled, letting the tension out of me. I'd freaked myself out for nothing.

I started the car and pulled around the driveway onto the main road. As I checked the rearview mirror, I swore I saw a light shining through a second-floor window. The electricity wasn't on yet, but it was scheduled to come on the following day. So, I decided it was nothing. The power company had just turned it on early. Strange, but not unheard of. At least I knew everything would be ready for us to start work in the morning. I pulled out of the driveway onto the road with confidence that Davida was right and that, no matter what, we'd restore the manor to its former glory with only the usual hitches along the way.

****

There's something charming about a bed and breakfast. The Valley Inn was no exception. It looked like a real-life gingerbread house, with its uneven shingle siding painted the loveliest shade of lavender and its massive wraparound porch. It was the picture of country charm. I walked up the sidewalk flanked with tulips. Plants hung from the porch, with their vines spilling over the edges of their pots. The owners, Mr. and Mrs. Xavier, sat on the porch swing, swaying back and forth. Mrs. Xavier, a plump, brown-skinned woman with full cheeks and a sunny demeanor, was in a red-flowered, short-sleeved frock with a cardigan draped over her shoulders. Mr. Xavier was her opposite, rail-thin with a stern face that looked like it would crack if he tried to smile too widely. He wore a straw fedora pushed way back on his bald head.

"How's it looking at Warner Manor?" Mrs. Xavier asked as I walked up the porch stairs. I hadn't told them I had bought the place, but they knew somehow. Gossip spread fast in these small towns.

"It looks rough, but I can't wait to start working on it." I walked up the steps, my legs feeling particularly heavy.

"That place has been an eyesore in this town for too long." Mrs. Xavier used her left foot to keep the swing rocking.

"I didn't think anyone would ever touch the place with all the rumors and—" Mr. Xavier stopped speaking abruptly and looked down at his leg, where his wife had poked him in the thigh with her index finger. "Don't you think she has a right to know what she's getting into?" he asked, his voice gruff. "She might as well know the truth." He let out a dry cough. "It's better for her to find out now while she still has time to back out of the deal and go back home." He stared at me like the suggestion that I leave would compel me to run away right then and there.

"The money has already left my account, and all the paperwork is signed, so it's a bit late for that." I jingled the house keys. I knew I probably shouldn't ask, but I couldn't resist. "What am I getting into?"

"Just be careful." The yellow porch light glinted in Mrs. Xavier's eyes.

"Be careful of what?" Was everyone in this town trying to scare me?

Mr. Xavier shook his head. "We don't want anything to happen to you."

Mrs. Xavier clucked her tongue but didn't say anything.

I wasn't certain, but Mr. Xavier's statement felt like a veiled threat. I stood in front of the door, watching him for a moment, trying to decide if I would call him out on it. I was tired and just wanted to change my clothes and get some food from somewhere, but I also wanted to know what was going on. The Xaviers were as good a resource as any. Turning my attention to Mr. Xavier, I asked, "So what are the rumors? Did Raoul sell his soul to the devil to be a world-famous painter or something?"

"Don't get him started." Mrs. Xavier got up. "I've got better things to do than sit out here and listen to foolishness." She nodded at me before going inside.

Mr. Xavier crossed his arms. "The problem with that place goes back a long time."

"How long?" I wanted to know what the locals believed, but that didn't mean that I would believe it too. I could tell from the tone of his voice that this was going to be a long story, so despite my hunger, I settled into the white wicker rocking chair next to the door. I needed to get off my aching feet, and it sure did feel good to sit down. The crickets chirped, sending their rhythmic song into the night.

Mr. Xavier cleared his throat. "People have added on to it over the years, but the original house was one of the first ones in this area."

"I know. It was built in 1752."

He creased his forehead when he looked at me as if displeased that I interrupted him. So, I decided to sit back and listen. "That's right. They say the people who built it, the Warners, were a wealthy family. The husband was looking for a bit of adventure in his life, so he was gone a lot. He fancied himself an explorer and would go on trips out west. He was probably one of those adrenaline junkies. That's what I think anyway. He left his wife and three children back at the house. They also had two enslaved people who stayed in the shack behind the manor. That shack has long since been torn down. Anyway, the way I always heard it was that the man of the house, Isaac Warner, came back from one of his adventures only to find everyone in the house dead, his wife, his kids, and the enslaved woman. It looked like they'd all killed themselves. I don't know the exact details, but some say the woman, Mary Warner, slit her babies' throats before cutting her own. The enslaved woman hanged herself in the shack."

"That's terrible." A horrifying image flashed in my mind that was so vivid it was like I'd seen the scene myself. Goosebumps rose on my arms.

"The enslaved man, John, was missing, and I'm sure you can guess how that ended. Of course, Warner decided John had something to do with all those folks dying, so he vowed to make him pay for the death of his family. I don't know how long it took to hunt him down, but eventually, Isaac and the other men in town found John hiding out in the woods. They beat him and hung from the old oak that used to stand in front of the house."

I was glad the tree wasn't there anymore.

"That old tree was cut down decades ago. Thank God."

"That's a horrible story."

Mr. Xavier grimaced. "It's not over yet. They left his body hanging in that tree for days, bruised, battered, and swollen beyond recognition. White folks would come by to gawk at it. Over time they noticed that instead of looking worse like a dead body should when it rots in the sun, John's body started looking better. It was like he was healing just hanging there. Then one morning, he was gone." Mr. Xavier passed his fingers in front of his face to demonstrate how he'd vanished.

"What happened?" I scooted toward the edge of my seat.

"Nobody knows. Most think somebody came and cut him down and buried him. Others say he came back to life and walked away." He grinned slyly.

I laughed at the notion. "What do you think?"

"It doesn't matter what I think. All that matters is that, ever since then, everyone who has lived in that house has met an untimely demise. That's why no one wanted to buy it." He pushed the swing back again with his toe, and the chain groaned.

I knew I shouldn't ask, but I wanted to hear more. "How?"

"Slit wrists, hanged, car wrapped around a tree." He listed these causes of death like he was making a grocery list.

"They all killed themselves?" I asked.

"Most did. Some deaths were considered accidental, but I have my doubts."

"Doubts?" I asked.

"There's something strange going on in that house. If I were you, I'd leave and never look back." He planted both of his feet on the ground, stopping the swing.

A balmy breeze blew over us, and I closed my eyes for a moment. Maybe I was too tired to eat. Maybe I just needed to go to bed.

"Looks like you've worn yourself out." I opened my eyes to see Mr. Xavier's hard stare fixed on my face.

"Yeah," I said. "There's so much work to do over there."

"You were there all day and didn't notice anything strange?" He raised his eyebrows at me.

The house did feel strange. I thought about the light that was on when I drove away but chose not to mention it. I didn't want to reinforce superstition. "Nothing at all. It's just an ordinary abandoned house."

He sat forward. "It takes time. Once you've been going there enough, you'll notice. It's best to leave before the curse attaches itself to you."

"I'm not going to do that. I have plans for that old house." I pushed up from the chair. "I have to clean up and get some rest."

"You do that. Have a good night. Most everything you need is in the room. There are restaurant menus in the nightstand in case you want to order some food."

I pulled the front door open. "You read my mind."

"No. I've just been running this place so long that I know what you need before you do," he said.

"Good night, Mr. Xavier."

He nodded his head at me. "Good night. Let me know if you see any ghosts."

"I definitely will." I chuckled.

CHaPTer 3

My suitcase sat open on the bed with the clothes spilling out of the sides. I still wasn't sure if I had packed too much or not enough. I was close enough to the city that if I really needed something from home, I could drive back to get it, but the whole point of staying here was to avoid that. The bed and breakfast was temporary. I rented the room because the photo was cute. I planned on staying for a few days before moving into the Airbnb I had reserved for the long haul. Though it required me to do a lot of work, this part of the trip could be like a mini vacation. Okay, I know I didn't think that part through. Hauling junk out of an abandoned house isn't what one does on vacation unless you're a weirdo like me. I didn't have to help with any of that stuff. I could've had Davida hire and manage the crew while I stayed at home, but this was what I loved. There was something deeply satisfying about turning a house into a clean slate that you could do anything with. Watching the beginning stages of the transformation is beautiful. I enjoyed giving something that was once discarded new life. There's also something fascinating about looking through all of people's old stuff to see what you can figure out about them from what they left behind. I was still hoping Raoul had left something valuable and tried to focus on that possibility to stay enthusiastic about the project. I'd become an expert at ignoring the restlessness that had settled in my chest as soon as I found out the house was mine.

My room at the Valley Inn was quaint, with the patchwork quilt draped over the bed and the Thomas Kinkade oil painting of a cottage on the wall. There was just enough room for a double bed and a little seating area. A worn oriental rug covered the dark hardwood floor. The built-in bookcase next to the bed housed a few mystery novels. Agatha Christie and Walter Mosely were prominently featured. The attached bathroom was small, with barely enough room for a stand-up shower, a toilet, and a sink. I wondered if it had originally been a closet.

I pawed through my clothes and pulled out a T-shirt and a pair of joggers. Realistically, I wasn't going to go anywhere to eat. I was too exhausted and needed to clean up and get some rest. My phone chirped as I headed into the bathroom to shower. I hesitated at the bathroom door, trying to decide whether or not to check it. I wasn't expecting to hear from anyone, but that made me curious. Usually, the only people who contacted me were related to work. When work hours ended, they went home to their families or had busy social lives. I only had work and *Law and Order: SVU*. I liked binge-watching as many episodes as needed to quiet my thoughts at night. I know it's strange that a show about rape, murder, and abuse would somehow make me feel safer. There is something about the way everything gets solved in the end, no matter how gruesome, that makes me feel like the world is okay.

Anyway, I checked my phone, hoping it wasn't bad news about the house.

"Are you ready yet?" the text message read. Bewildered, I stared at the screen. Ready for what? The number the message came from didn't make sense either: 888. Assuming it was spam, I deleted it and went to take my shower.

There's nothing better than a nice hot shower at the end of a day of grimy work. The musty smell of the house clung to me after spending the whole day there. I was happy to wash it away, but an ominous feeling enveloped me as I stood beneath the stream of hot water. Maybe I'd seen the movie *Psycho* one too many times. Fear spread over me slowly, turning my blood to ice. This sharp, steady sense of dread wasn't new to me. I'd always get it washing my face in the sink at night. A pit opens in my chest, and my stomach drops at the sudden thought that I'm not alone, even though I know I am—or should be. And though I couldn't say I heard anything through the sound of the shower, I felt like someone was in my room. I pictured them creeping into the bathroom, a knife held aloft. I peered out of the curtain, the water still drumming in the basin. Nothing. Just an empty bathroom. I wished I had closed and locked the bathroom door. Someone could be in my room, lurking just outside of my view. My imagination was clearly running away with me. Hurriedly, I rinsed off and grabbed a towel.

"Is someone there?" I asked as I wrapped the towel around myself and stepped out of the shower, knowing it was a stupid question. If someone were waiting in my room to murder me, they wouldn't answer. I tiptoed into the room, looking for my imagined intruder. No one was there. The room was empty. My suitcase lay on the bed with my clothes splayed across the patchwork quilt. The white curtains were drawn. I let out a sigh of relief.

Newly relaxed, I took my cosmetics bag from the bed and brought it into the bathroom to do my skin-care routine. I walked up to the edge of the sink, drying my shoulders with the corner of my towel, not even paying attention to what I was doing. I put the cosmetic bag down on the vanity next to the sink, and when I looked up, the number eight was scrolled in the steam on the bathroom mirror over and over again. I yelped and stepped back.

I pulled on some clothes and went in search of the Xaviers. There was no way I was going to spend the night there. I walked up the hallway on the second floor, where the other guest-room doors were all shut tight. Even though I hadn't seen any other guests, I could hear the gentle sound of snoring coming from one of the rooms. The television blasted from another. A conversation bled through another door. I wondered if every room was occupied. I hurried down the stairs to the living room. It was empty. A white ceramic lamp sat on the end table near the sofa, putting out a soft glow. "Mrs. Xavier?" I half whispered into the empty room.

A floorboard creaked somewhere, setting me on edge. "Mr. Xavier?"

"Is everything okay?" Mr. Xavier came out of the kitchen, a yellow-and-white checkered dish towel draped over his shoulder.

I rubbed the back of my neck self-consciously and looked at the floor. Forcing a strained smile, I said, "I'm just wondering if I can change rooms?" Suddenly, I felt ridiculous.

"Is there something wrong with your room?" His forehead creased.

I shifted my weight back and forth from one foot to the other, wishing I had thought up an explanation before making the request. "Well..." Even though I felt stupid, I decided the best thing to do was to go with the truth. "When I got out of the shower, something was written on the bathroom mirror in the steam. It kind of freaked me out. I'd feel better if I was in a different room."

He raised an eyebrow at me, the hint of a smirk playing across his face. "What was written on your mirror?"

I sighed. "The number eight over and over again."

He pulled the corners of his mouth down for a moment. "And you didn't write it?"

"Would I be standing here if I had written it?" I knew my request seemed ridiculous, but I didn't like being treated like I was a dummy. "Are there any empty rooms?" I hardened my voice.

"What's going on?" Mrs. Xavier rounded the corner.

"Ms. Jones would like to change her room." Mr. Xavier pointed his chin at me before giving his wife a knowing look.

"Oh dear, what's wrong with the room?" Her eyes widened.

"Nothing. I just feel uncomfortable there." Why did they need an explanation? Couldn't they just let me have another room?

"Why are you uncomfortable?" She exuded a motherly warmth as she stepped closer to me, and I longed for something I'd missed in life. She was so inviting that I felt I could tell her all my problems and cry in her arms.

"Somebody wrote eight over and over again on her mirror while she was in the shower." Mr. Xavier spoke like it wasn't a big deal at all. In fact, the way he downplayed it offended me.

"Which means that someone broke into my room while I was in the shower and wrote on the mirror." That explanation didn't make sense. There was no way anyone was in that room writing on the mirror. I would've seen them.

Mrs. Xavier sighed and crossed her arms over her ample chest. "You know what probably happened? Whoever was in the room before you wrote that on the mirror with their finger before they checked out. My brothers used to do that to me when we were kids. What happens is the oils from your finger get on the glass, and the mirror won't fog up in those spots when you take a shower. I must've forgotten to clean that mirror before you checked in."

Her explanation made sense. Were the numbers already on the mirror when I got out of the shower? They could've been. I didn't remember.

"We don't want to make you stay someplace you feel uncomfortable," Mrs. Xavier said. "Follow me. I'll set you up in a new room."

Her husband raised his finger and began to stammer a reply, but she hushed him.

"Putting her in another room is not a hassle, Douglas."

"I didn't say it was." But the way he shook his head and pursed his lips told me otherwise.

I lugged my hastily repacked suitcase up the hallway, following Mrs. Xavier. She opened the door of a room at the very end of the hall. "I hope you like this one."

I peered inside. It was a little bit smaller than the one I was in originally, but it had the same decor. The patchwork quilt lay sprawled across the bed. A landscape picture was on the wall above it. "It's not that I didn't like the first one," I said, feeling the need to explain myself. I didn't want them to think I was a picky princess. "I just felt unsafe because of the numbers on the mirror."

"Hopefully, this one doesn't have any numbers on the mirror," Mr. Xavier mumbled. He'd walked behind me with slow shuffling steps up the hallway. I wondered why he was still with us.

His wife gave him a playful shove. "Be kind to the guests." Her eyebrows drew together.

He sighed, turned, and walked up the hallway toward the stairs.

"Don't mind him." Mrs. Xavier waved her hand dismissively in his direction. "Some people get grumpy when they get old." She raised her voice to make sure he heard her.

"If I'm old, what are you?" he said without turning around. He continued to lope toward the staircase.

"Thank you so much. I'm sure this room will be fine." I wheeled my suitcase into the corner beneath the window. The curtain was open, but I couldn't see anything in the darkness, only my reflection in the glass. I reached up and drew the curtains closed. Then I turned around to see Mrs. Xavier standing in the doorway, looking at me.

"If you need anything else, don't hesitate to let either of us know," she said. "We want your stay here to be as comfortable as possible."

I walked over to the door and took the doorknob in my hand. "Thank you. I will." I started to push the door closed, but Mrs. Xavier continued to stand there, looking at me like she had something else to say. "Is everything okay?"

She parted her lips and then closed them again before shaking her head. "Everything is just fine. Have a good night." She turned to walk up the hall.

CHaPTer 4

I woke with a start from a deep, dark sleep. When I sat up, a piece of paper was stuck to my face, partially blocking my vision. I peeled it away to see that I'd left a giant glob of drool on a red-and-white Chinese takeout menu. The bedside lamp was on, and I still wore the exercise clothes I'd changed into after my shower. Takeout menus lay scattered across the bed. I looked at my phone to see the time—two eleven.

I needed to get back to sleep. I gathered the menus, discarding the drool-covered Chinese food menu in the trash can. As I stacked the pieces of paper, a chill ran down my spine. I got a distinct feeling that someone was watching me. I spun around, searching the room with my eyes. There was nothing amiss.

Once I saw a news report about people hiding cameras in hotel rooms and Airbnbs. What if there was a camera watching me now? I walked over to the dresser where the television sat and checked to make sure there were no cameras hidden there, but I didn't see anything suspicious. Could the remote control be a camera? I turned it over in my hand.

Then there was the bookshelf next to the window, filled with crime thrillers and mysteries. Could any of the books contain cameras? I pulled one out and flipped through the musty pages. It was a normal book. I slid it back on the shelf and grabbed another. Flipping through it gave the same result: just another ordinary book. I stood with my hands on my hips, wondering if I should go through them all when a cat yawled outside. The jarring sound broke me out of my paranoia. What was I doing? It was now two-thirty in the morning, and I needed to get to bed. I crawled beneath the covers in my exercise clothes. I didn't remember drifting off to sleep, but one rarely does.

***

When I pulled into the driveway, a giant gray dumpster sat on the front lawn. Davida's pickup truck was already parked on the side of the house. Even though she had a long drive, she'd managed to get there before me. My paranoid search of my room in the wee hours of the morning made me sleep in later than intended. I should've set an alarm.

As I got out of the car, two large sweaty men were carrying a dirty mattress out the front door. They tossed it into the dumpster with seemingly little effort. After they went back inside, Davida appeared on the porch, holding a black trash bag.

She pitched it into the dumpster before noticing me. "You finally decided to show up." She smiled as she wiped her hands on her pants.

"It's only nine-thirty." I nodded toward the house. "How's it going?"

"As good as expected."

"No surprises yet?" I asked.

Her eyes widened, and she drew in a sharp breath.

"Is that a yes?"

She grabbed my arm. "I have to show you something." She pulled me toward the front door. They had only been working since eight o'clock, and the debris had already been cleared away from the front entryway. In the living room, the discarded furniture was gone. Davida led me through the vast open room and up a dark side hallway.

"When will the electricity get turned on?" She casually flipped the light switch as she passed it, and nothing happened.

"I swear it was on last night." I remembered seeing the light glowing in the upstairs window when I backed out of the driveway.

"Well, it isn't on now." She pulled her flashlight from her pocket and aimed the beam at the darkened pot light in the ceiling.

"The bulb is probably blown out. Have you tried the outlets?"

She rolled her eyes. "No, I would've never thought of that." Her voice dripped with sarcasm. "Maybe I should try plugging something in to see what happens."

"Jeez, I was just checking." I decided against asking her about checking the circuit breakers and made a mental note to check them on my own.

"I found the electrical box. Nothing's been tripped. When the electricity comes on, it should work." Sometimes, I swore Davida could read my mind.

"I'll call the electric company and find out what's going on." Just as I finished that sentence, the light in the hallway flickered to life.

"About time." She turned off her flashlight and held her arms up and out as if welcoming a familiar friend. "Let there be light." She dropped her arms to her sides. "We have electricity," she called loudly, twisting around to project her voice into the main area of the house, but no one seemed to hear her.

"I had the weirdest night," I said to her. "It felt like I was being watched—like there was a camera in my room." We stood in the hallway under the bright light of the incandescent bulb.

"What? You found a camera in your room?" Her voice rose in volume.

"No, I just felt like someone was watching me."

She let out a loud exhale, and her body relaxed a bit. "Feeling like someone might be watching you is not the same as knowing someone put a camera in your room." She continued walking up the hallway, which seemed much longer than it should have been.

"I know. That's why I didn't say there was a camera in my room. I said that I felt like there was a camera in my room. Big difference." I sighed. Sometimes, I swore she was trying to misunderstand what I said. "When I got out of the shower, there was writing on the bathroom mirror."

"You mean in the steam?"

I nodded.

"My husband does that to me all the time. If you use your finger to write something on the glass, the oils from your skin keep those areas from fogging up." She walked up the hallway to the narrow door at the end.

"The lady who owns the bed and breakfast said that could've happened." I could imagine a pimply teenager in the bathroom writing the number eight over and over again on the mirror with his index finger. "You're right. Somebody else probably did that before I ever moved into the room."

Suddenly, I felt embarrassed that I had asked to change rooms and decided not to mention it to her.

She stood at the door now, waiting for me to catch up with her. "Then you saw it and got yourself all worked up, thinking someone was watching you." Amusement peppered her words.

"That's what happened. You're right." Her logical explanation eased my fears.

"But now you have an explanation, so there's no reason to worry."

"Right." I spoke softly, reassuring myself.

"Anyway, I wanted to show you this." She turned the old-fashioned glass doorknob, a relic overlooked by the interior designer who had updated the home for Raoul.

"What is it?" I asked. The door opened, revealing a pitch-black room.

Davida reached inside and felt along the wall for a light switch. I heard something click, once, twice, three times. "No lights in here." She took the flashlight in her hand and turned it on. The beam of light cut through the darkness, revealing stacks of dusty boxes that looked like they had not been touched in many years. One sat on the floor by the door. Davida reached in and grabbed it, dragging it out into the hallway.

"What's all this?" I came closer to get a better look.

"It's full of old newspapers." Davida folded back the panels, opening the box to show me the pile of yellowing newspapers. She pulled out the top one from the stack and held it up to me. "Look at this... 1925." She tapped the top of the front page with her flashlight. "And it's the *Portland Gazette*. There are boxes of them, all from different years and cities."

I took the paper from her, wondering why she was so eager to show it to me. "It looks like Raoul liked collecting old newspapers." I unfolded it, scanning the pages. My search was unconscious. I didn't even know what I was looking for until I found it. "Look here." I held the paper out for her to see.

She took it from me, careful not to damage the brittle pages. "Well, would you look at that? It looks just like Raoul, doesn't it?"

It certainly did. In the small black-and-white photo, Raoul sat on the ground next to the trunk of a large tree, his knees pulled up and a flat cap dangling from his fingers in front of his shins. His dark face seemed to be damp with sweat. He stared straight into the camera with defiance in his eyes. I looked over Davida's shoulder at the articles around the picture. None of them referenced it. There was one about healthy living. Another was an op-ed piece in which someone described the process he went through to become an American citizen. Another was a story about a child born with a previously unknown disease. None seemed to belong to Raoul's photo. "Isn't it strange that they would have the photo of a random black man in the middle of this paper with absolutely no explanation?"

Davida turned the page carefully as if doing just a little bit more reading would provide an answer. "Maybe this was supposed to be part of a giant art installation he never finished."

Glancing down at the photo again gave me chills. Part of me wanted to believe Davida's theory, but inside, I knew it wasn't the case. This was no art project. This was something else entirely. "I want your theory to be right, but I just don't believe it. There's something more going on here." I put the newspaper back in the box. "We don't have time to sort through this right now. We have a house to renovate." I spun around and headed back to the living room, eager to get to work. I didn't want to let on, but something about the picture of Raoul had unsettled me.

"What should we do with all of these then?" Davida called after me.

"Put them back in the room for now. I'll deal with them later." I wasn't sure what I would do with them. Even if I found pictures of Raoul in every single one, what would that mean in the long run? If more pictures of Raoul had been the only thing I'd found, that would've been fine, but once I did get around to looking through the boxes, nothing could've prepared me for what I did find.

CHaPTer 5

I kept thinking about the boxes of newspapers all day. The black-and-white photo of Raoul consumed my thoughts. After lunch, I couldn't hold back any longer. While everyone else worked, I sneaked into the back room Davida had shown me. Even though this was my house, and everything inside belonged to me, fear coursed through me as I walked up the long hallway that led to the room. The sound of everyone working faded into the background as I put one foot in front of the other, walking up the hallway that seemed to get narrower and narrower, longer and longer. I flipped on the light as I passed the switch. When I got to the door, I stood there for a few moments looking at it. Chilly air seeped through the crack around the door, sending the hairs on my arms standing on end. I took hold of the doorknob, and the coldness of it jolted me. Taking a deep breath, I turned it and pushed the door open. The hinges creaked, and I chuckled.

"Just like a scary movie," I whispered to myself, taking note of my pounding heart. I took one last look down the hallway, just in time to see one of the workers walk past the entrance carrying a two-by-four on his shoulder. I turned back around and almost expected to come face-to-face with Raoul. The thought scared me so much that I jumped, even though there was nothing there, only darkness.

I reached my arm in to flick on the switch, hoping that by some miracle, the lights were working. When they didn't, I pulled my arm out as quickly as possible. Usually, a dark room wouldn't scare me. Those sorts of things never did, but since last night I was skittish. Something about reaching into the darkness made me feel unsafe. Even though the house was supposed to be empty of squatters, I pictured someone hiding in the shadows waiting to grab hold of me. I pulled the flashlight from my pocket and turned it on. All I could see were dusty boxes stacked haphazardly. I couldn't tell how many there were. The one Davida had pulled out earlier rested at my feet in front of the door. Even though the photo inside seemed to call me, I was curious about the other boxes. Did they all contain newspapers? Did every newspaper hide a picture of Raoul somewhere inside its pages?

I didn't go far into the room, just enough to grab the closest box to the door. Hooking my hand inside the top, I dragged it out into the hallway.

I pulled the flaps open. The cardboard made a dull sound as it scraped against itself. A stack of yellowing newspapers stared up at me. I pulled out the top one and, holding the delicate paper in my hand, scanned the page. The title was printed in simple black letters at the top, *The Watchman and Southron*. This one was printed on September 14, 1911. My heart giddy with anticipation, I turned the pages. I didn't find him until the end, the second to last page. There he stood, looking glorious in a dark pinstriped suit. He held a slender black cane in his right hand, and a bowler hat sat on his head. He had the same arresting look I'd seen in the other photos. His mouth was clamped tight, tensing the muscles in his jaw. His eyes narrowed as he looked directly into the camera and directly into me. I scanned the articles around the picture, hoping to see something that mentioned him. There was an article about an unknown disease wiping out all of the trees in an apple orchard. Another about the winner of the local beauty pageant. Another about the mysterious death of local livestock. Nothing mentioned Raoul or explained why his picture appeared there.

I laid the paper on the floor beside me and picked up another. The date on the top of this one was 1923. The pages were smooth and less fragile than the last paper. The writing was so small and close together that it made the words on the page difficult to read. I wondered if people had better eyesight back then. I shifted, turning to lean against the wall as I held up the paper and unfolded it.

"Where are you, Raoul?" I said to myself. It had already become like a game. I scanned the first page and, not finding him there, opened it to the next. There he was, smack-dab in the center of the page. His dark eyes stared out at me. He wore a different outfit, a light-colored pair of pants and a sweater. A flat cap sat on his head. He looked to be the same age as he was in the other picture taken twelve years earlier. He looked the same in the picture I found in the attic.

I laid the paper out on the floor and examined the page. The words around the picture seemed to bleed together, making the articles almost impossible to decipher. The words didn't matter much to me anyway. I was most intrigued by the picture in the center of the page. I studied every detail of his face. How was what I saw possible? Intrigued, I reached over and pulled another paper from the pile in the box. I would look through every last one of them eventually.

"There you are." I turned around, nearly jumping out of my skin.

Davida stood behind me. Dirt streaked her jeans. Her face shone under a thin film of sweat.

"You almost gave me a heart attack." I grasped my chest dramatically.

"Didn't you hear me calling you? I've been looking all over the place for you." She looked at the stack of newspapers that had grown into quite an impressive pile next to me.

"I didn't hear you. I guess I was too wrapped up in..." I glanced down at the pile and noticed how large it was with some embarrassment. Then I realized how quiet the house was. "What time is it?"

"Six thirty. Everybody's gone home." She pulled her phone out of her pocket and looked down at it. "I have to get going. I've been looking for you for like twenty minutes." Her voice carried an edge of annoyance.

"Sorry. I was looking through these papers. There's a picture of Raoul in every one of them."

Davida raised an eyebrow. "I've been working my behind off, and you've been casually reading through old newspapers." She smirked, and I knew she wasn't really angry.

"Don't you think it's strange that there is a picture of him in all of them? These newspapers span almost a hundred years, and he looks exactly the same as he did in the seventies in every single one."

"Yeah, it's strange and creepy and all of that, but we've been through this already. He was an artist. These could be anything. Just because a newspaper says it's from 1910 doesn't really mean it is." She stood, looking down at me with her hands on her hips.

"I know, but I don't think that's what's going on here. I have a feeling that it's something else." I picked up the last newspaper I'd looked through and rubbed my thumb gently along the page. The paper had a silky quality that paper didn't have today.

"They can artificially age paper."

"I know, but this doesn't feel that way." I held the newspaper out for her to touch.

She reached out and petted the page awkwardly like she was petting a cat. "Whether or not it's creepy doesn't change the fact that we have a house to renovate. We're paying these guys and need to ensure everything gets done." She stopped speaking and looked at the floor, chuckling. "Listen to me. It's not like you're usually here for this part anyway. There's no reason for me to make a big deal of this, but I thought since you were here this time, it would be more like the old days. You know, when we had to do most of this stuff ourselves?" She shook her head.

"You're right. This is my dream project, and I said I would be here to help, so I should help." I looked at the stack of newspapers next to me. I'd wasted so much time.

"I'm sorry, Khadijah. I'm making this a bigger deal than it should be. I'm just a bit stressed out. This is the biggest project we've ever tackled, and there's the drive, and Donell's been having problems in school." She sighed.

"Oh no. What's going on with Donell?" I remembered the day he was born. It was hard to believe he was already twelve.

"You know how awkward he is. The kids in school have been picking on him." The happy tinkling of chimes came from her pants pocket. She took out her phone. "It's Jay." As she answered, she turned her back to me and walked up the hallway. "Hey, baby. No, I haven't left yet." She took the phone away from her ear and turned to look at me. "Are you okay here alone? I really need to go."

"Don't worry about me. Get home to your family." I waved my hand, shooing her.

"Good night. I'll see you tomorrow." She put the phone back to her ear and resumed talking as she disappeared around the corner into the living room. I could hear her footsteps on the tile, walking through the house and out the front door.

Davida was right. Raoul was known for his massive exhibits, but there were so many papers, and I hadn't even looked at them all. They all contained intricate details. He would've had to get so many articles written. And each newspaper had aged differently. It seemed like an impossible task, but the way Raoul made the impossible possible intrigued me. That was part of the reason why I loved his art in the first place. Yes, his giant canvases were bold, bright, and daring, but what impressed me most was the large installations he did on buildings in New York City; many of them were installed in secret under the cover of the darkness, like the mural of the woman that stretched the entire height of the ten-story building in Manhattan. One day, the wall was dirty gray and ordinary, and the next morning, it was covered with the most fantastic work of art. A regal African woman looked out over the city. Up close, she looked like a series of bright dots. She only became visible from a distance. An intricate red wrap sat on her head. Her angular brown face looked out from the brick as if ready to pass judgment on anyone who stepped before her. Her tomato-red dress billowed out, transitioning to a river of blood. I wished I'd seen the painting in person before the building was torn down in the 1980s.

I was sitting on the floor thinking about how he could've made that amazing work of art happen when I realized how quiet it was. I was completely and utterly alone. Not bothering to put the newspapers back in their box, I got up and walked up the narrow hallway to the living room. I had been occupied all day and hadn't seen how much work had gotten done. The living room was empty, and part of the drywall was torn away on one side. I couldn't make out much in the dim light, so I went to the other side of the room and turned on the tall construction lamp. The floodlight hummed with electricity, filling the entire space with white light that was almost too bright. It was so much easier for me to picture my vision for this place with all of the garbage from the past gone. My anxiety had settled down since the work had started. We had so much to do, but I could already see the potential here. I imagined clean marble floors, freshly plastered walls, and a chandelier hanging from the tall ceiling. I could already picture the wide-open space filled with people gathered for an event. I didn't have any of Raoul's art to display here yet. That would have to come with time. I'd naively hoped that I'd find something of his abandoned in the house. So far, that hadn't happened. I was imagining how I might get an art collector to donate some of his pieces to be displayed in the house when a sudden noise pulled me out of my dreams.

Something crashed to the floor, making a mighty clanging sound somewhere upstairs. I jumped, my heart hammering in my chest. My intuition told me to leave the house, but I couldn't. This was my house now and my responsibility. What if the squatters who had been staying here had returned? I pulled my phone from my pocket and wondered if it was too soon to call the police. What if I had only heard an animal?

I spotted a hammer lying on the floor and picked it up. The heft of it in my hands gave me a sense of power. Surely, if I were attacked, I could use it as a weapon. My aim was pretty good; if I had to throw this at someone's head, I think I would hit it.

I heard another sound, like marbles rolling across the floor, directly above me. Do you know how in movies, when people hear sounds and they should be alone, they always call out? I never understood that. If a thief is in your house, don't you want the element of surprise? Shouldn't you sneak up on them? That was my plan. I tiptoed through the living room and up the hall that led to the entryway. The staircases, though still in disrepair, were clear of debris now. Hugging my body against the wall, I approached the staircase to my left. I crept up the stairs to the second floor. Silence had once again descended upon the house, causing me to doubt myself for a few minutes. Had I heard anything at all? Then I thought I heard footsteps somewhere upstairs, out of sight in the darkness. Knowing that pulling out my flashlight and flicking it on would warn anyone roaming around the second floor of my approach, I chose to navigate the darkness. Staying close to the wall and keeping my breath even, I stepped forward. My breathing was fast and shallow even though I tried desperately to control it. I was doing it all wrong. As I started down this path, I knew it. I had turned into one of those women in the horror movies doing all the wrong things, but still, I propelled myself forward, my fingertips touching the wall, hoping I wouldn't trip on anything. I did my best to quiet my breathing and ignore the rapid thumping of my heart. Surely, whoever was squatting here wasn't that dangerous. That's what I told myself at least.

I crept further into the darkness, holding my breath intermittently. It was my feeble attempt at being even quieter. The whole time I listened. Every creak of the floorboard, every whisper of the wind outside, every chirp of the cricket drew my attention. As I slid my feet along, the side of my foot came in contact with something solid. My heart raced, and my imagination ran away with me. I could picture so clearly in my mind a man standing in the dark watching me, mocking me in my moment of terror. What had I gotten myself into? The fear rose in my throat as the sense of being watched increased. Even though I didn't hear footsteps, I swore someone was walking up to me. The presence pushed in on me until I couldn't take it anymore.

"Who's there? Get back!" I swung the hammer out in front of me with one hand as I reached into my pocket with the other and pulled out my flashlight. "Stay back, or I'll hit you!" My voice strained, and my body tensed. I fumbled with my flashlight, trying desperately to turn it on without dropping it. Finally, I turned it on, and a white beam sliced through the darkness, illuminating the dirt-streaked wall in front of me. I twisted, shining the light around me as quickly as I could, trying to catch a glimpse of whoever was there with me. As I did, I lost my balance and stumbled over what I had been standing next to. Landing on the floor with a loud thud, I dropped the hammer but managed to hang onto my flashlight. Panic coursed through me. I swung the flashlight around, looking for what I had fallen over. A brick lay on the floor beside me. I felt foolish. Convincing myself that what I heard was only the house settling or, more likely, falling apart, I found my way to my feet and shined my flashlight down the hallway. Listening, I only heard the sounds from outside again: wind and crickets. I had just begun to relax when I heard another noise, the sound of someone running. It seemed to come from the room right near the staircase. Shining my light up the hallway, I ran toward the room. "You can't be in here!" I called. It was coming from the room where the squatters had been, and I assumed they were back. I dashed into the room, shining my light around, only to see an abandoned sneaker caked with mud in the middle of the floor. No one was there, but the window was wide open.

I listened. There was no sound. In my mind, I could picture someone crouching down in a dark, shadowy corner, waiting for me to leave. I shone my light around the room and saw something familiar sitting against the wall. My heart pounded in my chest as I walked toward it. The wind blew through the window, and a bit of moonlight trickled in. A man's dress hat sat on the floor. It hadn't been there before, and I couldn't imagine one of the builders having it and leaving it here. I walked right up to it, aware that my back was to the door, and even though I knew the foolishness of it, I was too fascinated not to examine it. Bending down, I looked at the hat more closely. It seemed brand-new, not dusty and worn like everything else in this house. How did it get there?

"Is anyone here?"

Silence answered me. I left the hat and went over to the window to look out. Again, I saw nothing unusual, only the view across the overgrown garden. The moon hung low and round in the sky. "There's no one here, Khadijah. Just relax," I told myself. I shined my flashlight around the room one last time. This time, facing a different direction, I caught sight of something else. Sloppy, dripping, red letters were scrawled across the old graffiti on the wall. "Welcome home."

CHAPTER 6

I backed away from the wall, shaking my head. Who could've written this? I ran out the door and tore down the staircase, the beam of light from my flashlight bouncing as I went. When I got to the front door, I yanked it open and ran outside. A car turned into the driveway, the headlights blinding me. It stopped just behind my car as I dug into my pocket for my keys. I could hear myself squealing with fear, but I had no control over it. Standing at my car door, I continued to try to pull my keys from my pocket, but somehow, they were stuck. Then I felt a hand on my shoulder, and I spun around, ready to hit the person behind me. To my surprise, it was Alton. His eyebrows knit together with worry.

"Khadijah, calm down. What's going on?"

When I saw him, the fear drained out of me. My shoulders relaxed. "I was just in the house, and I swear someone was in there with me."

He looked at the house. "I'll check it out." He went back to his car and opened the glove box. He came out with a gun. The dark metal shone in the moonlight.

I gasped. I'd never seen a gun in real life before. "Why do you have that?"

He shrugged. "You never know when you might need it."

"You need to be careful. It could get you killed," I said.

"Don't worry. I'm careful." He walked toward the front door. "Is it locked?"

I was so busy trying to run away that I hadn't thought of locking it. "No."

"Do the lights work?" He walked up onto the porch.

"Some of them. There is a construction light on in the living room. What I heard was upstairs though, and there's no lights up there." Remembering my flashlight, I looked around. I was no longer holding it. "I think I dropped my flashlight by the door when I opened it."

He crept up to the door, holding his gun like the police do on TV. Then he pulled the door open. "I have a gun. Come out now with your hands up if you don't want me to shoot you." He pointed it into the house. While still pointing the gun with one hand, he crouched down and picked up my flashlight. Then, he waited by the door for someone to make an appearance.

Nothing happened.

"I'm going inside." He stepped into the house.

I looked around me. The moon was only a crescent hanging above me, and bright stars freckled the sky. Suddenly I realized that I was standing alone in the driveway in the dark in the countryside. Maybe I would be safer with Alton because he did have the gun. Or maybe I should lock myself in the car. I convinced myself that was a better option. If anything happened, I could call the police. "Okay," I called to him. "I'm going to wait here. I hope you don't mind." I finally pulled the keys from my pocket and hit the button to open my car.

I sat in the car watching the house, well aware of how alone I was. I must have checked that the doors were locked three times. I pulled my phone from my pocket and kept it resting unlocked on my lap so I could call 911 quickly. Looking at the house, I could see the beam from the flashlight through the windows on the second floor as Alton moved around the house. I listened for gunshots and hoped he would be okay. He was only gone for less than ten minutes, but it felt like an eternity. Finally, he emerged and came over to the car. I rolled down the window and glanced at the gun at his side. Noticing the direction of my gaze, he stuck it in the waistband of his pants.

"I don't think there's anybody in there, but it's hard to tell. There are so many places where someone could hide." He handed the flashlight to me.

"That's not reassuring." I looked up at the old house.

"I know. But it's the best I can do." He bit his lip. "I saw the new graffiti."

I nodded. Just thinking about it made me tear up. "So did I. That's why I was so freaked out."

"Maybe someone wants to scare you out of town." He looked down at me with his dark eyes.

"But why would someone want to do that?"

He shrugged. "You would probably know better than me."

But I didn't know. "Maybe whoever was squatting in the house is still there."

"I guess it's a possibility. In the future, you shouldn't hang around here alone at night. It's not safe."

"You're probably right." I was in such a state when he showed up that I didn't really know what I was doing. I was grateful for his help. "What were you doing here this late anyway?"

He shrugged again and looked at the ground for a moment. "I was driving by and thought I'd check to see if anyone was here. I was just curious about how things were going."

"Curious?" I searched his face.

"Yeah." He looked at the dumpster outside the front door. "And I wanted to check on you, that's all."

"Who says I need checking on?"

He let out a little laugh. "From what I saw when I pulled up, it looks like you do. I was just being gentlemanly." He backed away from the car. "You look like you're still pretty shaken up. Are you okay to drive?"

Was I okay to drive? I looked down at my shaking hands. My heart pounded in my chest. I could hear the blood rushing in my ears. "Yeah, I can manage," I lied. I wasn't sure I could manage anything at the moment, but I'd spent most of my life pretending I had it all under control.

He pursed his lips, the corners of his mouth drawing down. "Are you sure? It's not a big deal for me to give you a ride."

I pushed the ignition button to start my car. The purr of the engine was almost imperceptible. "I'll be fine. I don't want to be a bother."

"I wouldn't have offered if it was too much of a bother." He blinked slowly. "Text me when you get to your bed and breakfast, so I know you got there okay."

"I will," I said. I sat in the car, waiting until Alton got into his car and started it before I drove away. The gravel crunched under our tires as we pulled around the circular driveway. I turned right, and Alton followed me. The country road was so dark it seemed dangerous.

"Don't they believe in streetlights around here?" I asked myself as I took my time, driving up the dark road.

Because Alton was behind me, I checked my rearview mirror a little too often, wondering how far he would be following me. One minute, I checked the mirror, and his headlights were still there; the next moment, they were gone. I suddenly felt very much alone. The road beneath my headlights seemed darker than any I'd ever seen. It twisted and turned through farmland. I squinted and leaned forward against my steering wheel as I drove. I checked my headlights several times to ensure they were working because even when I put on the high beams, it didn't make a difference. There were no other cars, and after driving for what felt like quite a while, I started to wonder if I'd missed my turn. Was I going the wrong way? I reached over to grab my phone off the passenger seat. I'd only looked away for a few moments, a split second if that, when I hit something. My car veered off the road into a field of tall grass.

My heart racing, I sat in the car, gripping the steering wheel. What had I hit? I looked in the rearview mirror and could only see blackness behind me. I put my car in reverse and backed up a few feet. I was considering just driving away and pretending nothing had happened, but my conscience talked me out of it. I'd have to go out to the road to check. I put the car in park, opened the door, and got out. I went around to check the front to see how much damage there was to my car. I'd never had an accident in a rental before and had no idea how to deal with it. I just hoped the car was fine. The headlights were blindingly bright, but I thought I saw a streak of blood on the left side of the hood. Then I heard a groan of pain coming from somewhere behind me. I grabbed my flashlight from the car before walking through the grass to the road. I shined the beam of light in front of me, afraid of what I might see. A dark crimson streak smeared the asphalt. The metallic smell of fresh blood filled my nostrils. I could hear the scraping on the road so close to me, but I was too afraid to shine the light in that direction. I had no idea what I might see and wanted to protect myself from the horror of it all. Slowly, I followed the track of blood, raising the beam of light to where an animal lay, half of its body crushed to the road and the top half still conscious and moving. It whined as it twisted its head back and forth in an unnatural motion that almost seemed like a video playing backward. At first, I couldn't make out what it was, and then it turned its head toward me, and I could tell it was a coyote. It tried desperately with its front legs to pull itself across the asphalt, but it couldn't move. I yelped and turned, running back to my car. I got in and slammed the door closed. Even in the safety of my car, I could hear the animal howl in pain. I couldn't just drive away and leave it. I had to do something. I threw the car into reverse and backed out to the shoulder of the road. Sitting on the shoulder, I looked up the street and saw no cars were coming, and then I looked in my rearview mirror: still nothing. All I could see around me was total blackness. The pleading of the injured coyote seeped into my car, cutting through my heart. I hoped another vehicle would come along soon and put the animal out of its misery, but how long would that take? I had to do something.

I backed up some more so I could see the animal in my headlights yowling in the road. I put the car in drive, took a deep breath, and put my foot on the accelerator. I felt its body under my tires, a soft bump. Then I slammed on my brakes. Unsure of whether or not it was dead, I put my car into reverse and ran over it again. Then I put on my brakes, and I saw it—a mass of matted fur and pink flesh on the blacktop. There was no way it was alive now. I put my car in drive and drove over it one last time.

Adrenaline pumped through me as I drove. I put on the radio, looking for something happy to listen to, and I tried not to cry while driving down the road. I didn't usually listen to the radio but wanted a distraction to pull the terrible image from my mind. When I turned the radio on, it was silent at first, and I thought it was broken. I went to change the station, but just before my finger hit the button, a man began to speak.

"Wait," the deep disembodied voice said. It was like he was talking to me directly.

I froze, wondering what he would say next. It didn't take long before he spoke again.

"It is natural to try to draw conclusions from this. You want to believe that you can see, taste, feel, and hear all this world is made of. We get comfort from the idea that everything around us is as we perceive it to be. But is that really the case? Before you make assumptions about Kathy's story and whether or not she is out of her mind, think about what's real. And how you can really know." I listened as if he was talking directly to me.

A woman started to talk. Her voice was muffled and sounded like she was not in the studio but talking on the telephone. "Thank you, Evan. I appreciate what you said. I don't usually share this story because people think I'm crazy. I used to think I was crazy until I met other people who'd experienced the same thing. This happened. It happened to me. And no matter if you believe it or not, it doesn't change the facts." The woman spoke with resolve.

"Tell our listeners your story, Kathy," Evan said.

Kathy cleared her throat again. "Pardon me. I'm a bit nervous."

"Don't be," Evan said. His voice was calm.

Kathy sighed.

"Take as long as you need to. It's only the radio." He chuckled. "Do you want me to go to a break, and then we'll continue your story when we come back?"

"N-n-no," Kathy stuttered. "I'm fine." She paused again.

I leaned forward, so full of anticipation that I almost forgot to pay attention to the road. The headlights lit the path only yards in front of me. I hadn't seen another car for what felt like forever, but none of that mattered. I was focused on Kathy and the story she had to tell.

"My husband was no ordinary man. I had a suspicion from the beginning. If I trusted myself, I would've found out before I did, but when it comes to things like this, it's hard to trust yourself. Once I realized, I confronted him."

Evan interrupted Kathy. "We need the listeners to understand what was going on. I know you like to skip ahead, but I need to make sure you tell the listeners out there what happened exactly." I could picture him leaning forward with his chin on his fist, eager to hear her story. "Start from the beginning."

Kathy cleared her throat. "My husband had another life." Her voice quivered. "I don't mean he was cheating or had some other family in another town. I mean, he had another life hundreds of years before he met me. He had multiple lives in multiple places because he could live forever."

"So, what you're saying is that your husband was a vampire?" Evan asked.

"Nooo." The way she said it let me know that she thought the idea of vampires was ridiculous, just like I did. "Not in the typical 'I want to suck your blood'"—she put on a funny voice like she was in an old fashion movie—"kind of way." She paused and swallowed so loudly that I could hear it. "At least, I don't think so. He was something else, something worse than a vampire. Vampires are just imaginary stories, but he was my husband."

"Okay, Kathy. You need to give us some more details here. How did you meet your husband?"

"It was nothing extraordinary—" Static broke in as the signal began to fade. "We dated—" More static. "He was such a good—" And more static.

Frustrated, I smacked the steering wheel with my open hand. I was so drawn into Kathy's story that I nearly forgot how scared I'd been.

"Even though—" I heard a few static-filled words from her, then it cut out again.

I waited, hoping the signal would come back. Kathy's story had completely melted away into static. I fiddled with the radio, trying to get the signal back. I turned the channel and ended up on a station playing Christian rock. Then I turned back to the channel I was listening to before, and it was still static. I tried again and got salsa music. And again, more static. Frustrated, I left the button alone. The drone of white noise filled the car and canceled out my anxious thoughts. I hoped the station would come back in, and I would hear some of Kathy's story. I turned down the radio so the static was audible over the sound of my tires on the road but not too annoying. It was like a cradle of noise there to hold my attention and keep me from thinking too much about everything that had happened so far.

With the static still playing gently beneath my thoughts, I turned right up the winding tree-lined road that led to the bed and breakfast. In the darkness of night, there wasn't much to see, but during the day, the street was gorgeous. I loved how the road narrowed in spots, allowing the branches to meet overhead to form a living tunnel. It was like something from a travel brochure in daylight, and at night, it was more like something from a horror movie. At least the area was a bit more populated, and finally, I saw some cars pass me going the other direction. I wasn't all alone in this world after all. I looked at the dashboard clock as I rounded the bend just before the turn into the bed and breakfast parking lot. The static on the radio was oddly calming. It played in my mind, releasing all the tension and fear I felt that evening. I never understood before why anyone would listen to white noise, but now I kind of got it. I parked the car and was reaching down to turn off the ignition when I swore I heard a voice say my name on the radio. It was almost masked by the static, but it was there. Amongst the noise, a deep, almost electronic-sounding voice said, "Khadijah." I looked down at the radio, my eyes wide with shock.

"What?" I said aloud.

"Khadijah." It repeated my name as if it had heard me.

The blood drained from my face, and my body went cold. The voice, though distorted, sounded familiar. Something in my subconscious began to stir. A lump rose in my throat. I swallowed it down. Tears stung the corner of my eyes. "What's happening?" I asked aloud. Part of me was just talking to myself, but part of me was asking the voice on the radio.

"You already know." The words dropped off. I turned up the volume, and the static blasted into the car.

"Already know what?" I whispered, looking down at the radio.

I waited for an answer, but none came.

I hit the button on the radio, turning it off. The silence broke the spell. In my quiet car, I looked up at the bed and breakfast. The porch light glowed yellow. A tall oak stood next to the porch, its branches reaching high overhead. There were only three other cars in the parking lot, and they were empty. I was the only one sitting in my car in the dark, slowly losing my mind.

CHAPTER 7

I was still feeling disoriented when I entered the bed and breakfast. A young couple sat on the sofa in the front room, talking to each other in hushed tones. The woman pushed her blonde hair back behind her shoulder and laughed at something the man said. Soft jazz played from a speaker in the corner. I felt like I was interrupting an intimate moment, so I hurried through the room and up the stairs.

I just wanted to go to my room, but Mr. Xavier was standing in the hallway.

"How are you doing?" he said as I approached.

"Good, thanks." There was no point in telling him anything else.

He looked at me like he didn't believe me. "Are you happy with your new room?"

"Yup." I took out my key and unlocked my door.

"Hmmm." He crossed his arms over his chest and narrowed his eyes at me like he didn't believe me.

I bit my tongue to keep from saying anything rude. There was no reason to be snarky. "Good night," I said, putting on my sweetest voice.

I went to push the door closed, but Mr. Xavier cleared his throat. "Have you found anything over in that house?" He shifted a bit, and I realized that his posture wasn't defensive. It was more like he was hanging onto himself for dear life. I could picture him dropping his arms to his sides and his body suddenly blowing apart. Mr. Xavier looked like a man trying desperately to hold himself together.

I wasn't sure what he was getting at but decided to play along. "Like what?"

He drew the muscles of his face in, puckering his lips slightly and deepening the lines between his eyebrows. "You'll know when you see it."

I narrowed my eyes at him. "I did find something strange. Maybe you know something about it."

He took a step toward me, interested. "What's that?"

I drew in a deep breath and exhaled slowly. "There are boxes and boxes of newspapers in the house. The dates on them go back more than a hundred years."

I watched his face for his reaction to this first statement, but his expression was neutral.

"Anyway, there are pictures of Raoul in every single newspaper. He always looks the same, just like he did in the seventies at the height of his career." I paused, waiting for a reaction. When he didn't give one, I continued. "I figure it's probably some kind of art project, you know, something he kept secret."

"That's a theory." His expression tightened. "Not the most likely one, but it definitely is a theory." He turned as if he was done with me and started walking away.

Still holding the doorknob, I stepped forward out of my room. I wasn't ready for him to go yet. "What's your theory?"

He stopped and thought for a moment. "Who says I have one?" He shrugged and continued walking away. "You can still leave. You know that, don't you?" He didn't turn around to look at me when he spoke.

"I can't," I said to his back.

"Yes, you can." He stopped mid-step as if considering saying something else.

"What do you know?" I asked, taking another step out of my room.

"Nothing." He didn't turn to face me. Instead, he hung his head, revealing his thin neck. "Goodnight. Sleep well." He continued walking away from me.

Part of me wanted to go after him, but I was tired and on edge. I let him go down the hallway to the stairs which creaked under his weight as he descended them.

I didn't realize how hungry I was until I entered my room. I collapsed onto the bed. My body ached with exhaustion. My mind raced, and my stomach growled. I'd gone all day without eating. I was so engrossed in looking through the newspapers that I hadn't even stopped for lunch. I knew that if I didn't eat something, I wouldn't get any sleep. So, I fished out the restaurant menus in the nightstand drawer.

I was about to order a pizza when my phone rang. It was Alton. I answered quickly, realizing that I'd forgotten to text him.

"Hi. I'm sorry. I totally forgot."

He chuckled. "I thought so. I was just checking to make sure you got back okay."

"Yep. I'm here safe and sound."

"Good." He paused. "I hope you don't mind, but one of my friends is a cop, and I told him about what happened. He offered to stop by the house tomorrow to check it out for you."

"Thank you."

"It's dangerous for you to be there alone, especially if someone is getting in somehow."

"Maybe I should get a gun." I laughed even though the thought of having one gave me chills.

"Maybe you should." He sounded so serious that I regretted suggesting it.

"I was just kidding."

"I wasn't," he said.

"It's okay. I have pepper spray." I thought of the metal canister in my suitcase that I'd kept forgetting to take to the manor.

"That's a start. To be safe, don't hang out around there alone at night anymore."

His concern made me smile. "Alton, thanks for worrying about me, but I'll be fine."

I heard someone else talking in the background. "I have to go." Something scraped against the mouthpiece of his phone. I heard a muffled conversation. He was talking to someone, but I couldn't make out the words. "I've really got to go. My friend will be over tomorrow morning."

"What?"

"The cop to check the place out."

"Okay. Thanks." I wondered where he was and who he was with. Was he dating anyone? Was he married? I had no idea.

"Okay. Bye." He hung up so abruptly that it was shocking.

I sat, looking down at the phone, my stomach rumbling. The muffled music from downstairs drifted up through the floorboards. It was early, but I was so mentally exhausted that I felt like I could curl up and sleep for days. The air in the room was heavy, and I didn't know if it was the space itself or just me, but a sense of gnawing dread pushed at me. My phone vibrated in my hand. I looked down at the screen, expecting to see a text from Alton. Instead, I saw the number eight repeated over and over again. My heartbeat quickened, knocking against my sternum. When I looked to see who had sent the text, the phone number read 888-8888. "This has to be a prank," I told myself.

It was the only logical thing to think. Why would the same numbers written on the mirror in my room last night appear on my phone today? Someone was trying to make me feel like I was crazy. And they were succeeding.

My stomach rumbled, and I didn't want to stay in this room for another moment, so I grabbed my purse and keys. Despite being exhausted, I'd go somewhere to have dinner. Hopefully, a good meal would chase away the uneasy feeling that wouldn't leave me alone.

Chapter 8

The following morning, I pulled into the driveway at Warner Manor early. No one else was there yet, and the events of the night before made me reluctant to go inside alone. So, I sat in my car reading my emails until a police cruiser pulled into the driveway. A handsome young officer got out. He was tall, dark-skinned, square-jawed, and probably way too much trouble for someone like me. He looked up at the house, squinting into the sunlight. I got out of my car and did my best to seem calm, cool, and collected.

"Hello. You must be Alton's friend. Thank you for coming." I walked confidently toward him, aware that I wanted to make a good first impression. When doing a project like this, it's always helpful to be on the good side of the police. When I first started, I had several instances of squatters breaking into the homes I was fixing up and stealing things. Those were much smaller projects in more heavily populated areas, but this home had attracted attention over the years.

He shook my outstretched hand firmly. "I'm Devin Moses."

"Khadjah," I said. "It's great to meet you."

He looked at the house again. "Alton said you're having a problem with squatters."

"Yeah, they were in there last night." I kept telling myself that it was just squatters, even though I was starting to think something more sinister was afoot.

"Have you gone inside yet this morning?" He was doing me a favor, and there was no time to stand around making small talk.

"Not yet. I was hoping you would come in with me and check it out. Just in case." I walked quickly to the front door, pulling the key from my pocket. He followed me.

"It's a beautiful place, isn't it?" he said behind me.

I stuck the key in the lock. "That's why I bought it."

"You're not exactly what I pictured when I heard someone had bought this place. I thought it would be developers."

I turned and looked back at him. "I am a developer." I pushed the door open.

"You know what I mean." He cleared his throat. "Well—" He never finished his thought. "I'll just take a quick look around." He went into the house before me and headed toward the living room.

"They've been staying upstairs. That's where I saw someone last night." I pointed up the most stable staircase. "You better use that one."

He nodded. "Sure thing." He started up the stairs, and I stood awkwardly, wondering if I should follow him.

Just then, I heard a car outside. Looking out the door, I saw Davida's truck pull up. "My partner is here."

"I'll find you when I'm done." He went up the stairs a lot faster than I would've, considering the state of them.

Once he was out of sight, Davida appeared in the doorway.

"What happened?" Her forehead creased.

"What do you mean?" I asked.

"The police are here." She looked around, searching for evidence of the officer.

"Oh." I'd forgotten that she didn't know. "I thought I saw someone upstairs last night. He's checking to see if anyone is still hanging around."

Davida headed for the stairs. "Where? What did they look like?"

"In the room with the graffiti." I followed her up the stairs even though I didn't really want to. After last night, the second floor had an ominous feeling.

"He's just looking around," I said as I followed her.

"I know, but this is our place. We need to know what's going on. If he finds something, I want to be there." Her voice bounced as she went up the stairs. I let Davida go into the room with the graffiti on her own. I couldn't even stand getting too close to the doorway. A small section of the room entered my line of sight, and I could already see that the graffiti had changed. The number eight was written over and over again on the walls in dripping red spray paint.

Davida turned to look at me, her mouth agape. "Someone's definitely been busy."

My heartbeat quickened, rattling against my rib cage. I approached the door and peered inside the room. "Oh my God." I held my hand to my mouth.

"Are you okay?" Davida looked over at me. "It's not that bad. We just have to make sure they don't get in again."

I heard heavy footsteps in the hallway and grabbed Davida's arm.

"Khadijah, are you up here?" It was Officer Moses.

"Yeah, in here," I replied.

He appeared in the doorway, and we both turned around. "This is Davida." I motioned toward her as I introduced them. "Davida, this is Officer Moses."

He gave a slight nod of acknowledgment before turning his attention back to me. "Well, you've definitely had a visitor."

Davida motioned to the graffiti on the walls. "We can see."

"This wasn't here before either?" He looked around at the walls.

"What do you mean by either?" I spoke slowly, afraid of what his answer might be.

He shook his head. "In the room back there, you have two dead cats. It looks like something was eating them."

"Jesus." Davida held her hand to her chest and looked at me with wide eyes. "What would do that?"

"I'm no wildlife expert. Maybe a coyote or a raccoon," he said.

"Do coyotes and raccoons graffiti walls too?" I joked. Lightening the mood was the only way to keep me from having a breakdown right then.

He snorted. "That is definitely the work of a human."

"Maybe they killed the cats too," Davida said.

"It's possible. I see people do all kinds of deranged things." He paused for a minute as if thinking. "It looks like they're getting in back here." He left the room and started up the hallway. We followed him back to the last bedroom, which was so small it was more like a glorified closet with windows. "Look here." He pointed to a broken window in the back corner where the glass was completely gone. "It would be easy for your squatter to climb up the trellis to this roof and come in through this window." He pointed at the wooden trellis running up the side of the house, thickly overgrown with ivy. "Board this up, and you can stop them from coming in for a while at least." He looked satisfied as he turned around and looked at us. "It might be worth it to get an alarm system."

"I can't believe we didn't notice that before," Davida mumbled under her breath.

"The best strategy for now is to keep whoever is coming in out," he continued. "Unfortunately, I can't do anything about it, but at least you know."

"Thank you," I said quickly. "What you've done so far has been great. If I'd found this on my own, I would've been freaked out."

We walked him downstairs and out the front door.

"Call me if you need anything else," he said before leaving.

"Well, let's get that window boarded up, and hopefully, we won't have any more problems." Davida went back into the house just as two pickup trucks pulled into the driveway. The crew was arriving. I hoped I could convince one of them to clean up the dead cats upstairs because I definitely didn't have the stomach to do it. JJ got out of his cherry-red pickup truck. "Morning, Khadijah."

"Morning." I spoke weakly, still feeling sick from what I'd seen upstairs. "Could you do me a favor?"

He raised an eyebrow as if reluctant to say yes. "What?"

"Wise man. Always find out what people want to do before you say yes." I smiled weakly. "Somebody broke in last night and killed some cats upstairs. I don't have the stomach to clean them up. I know it's a terrible thing to ask you to do but..."

"There are some sick people out there." JJ shook his head. "Don't worry about it. I'll clean it up."

I saw a blood-soaked paw sticking through a hole in the garbage bag when JJ passed me on his way to get rid of cats. I didn't ask what he did with them. I didn't want to know. I did my best to stay busy to keep my mind off what had happened.

I walked through the debris of the house, heaving a box of newspapers.

"What are you doing with that?" Davida asked, wiping her hands on her jeans.

I shifted a bit, trying to balance the heavy box on my hip. "I thought I'd take this back to my Airbnb to look through it." Just as the box started to slip from my hands, JJ came by and took it from me.

"Where are you going with this?" He held the box like it weighed nothing.

"To my car." I gave my tired arms a shake, grateful for the help.

"Let's get them out there then." He walked through the living room and out the front door.

"I want to look through them tonight."

"Knock yourself out." Davida pulled her phone from her pocket and looked at it.

"How's Donell?" I asked.

Davida shook her head. "Hardheaded. You know how they are at that age. He thinks he knows everything."

I didn't really know. I had no children of my own, and I didn't really remember my teenage years. Much of my childhood was a blur. My therapist thinks that childhood trauma made me forget my past. That is possible. The few scattered early memories I did have weren't good.

JJ came bounding back into the house. I wondered how he still had so much energy after working all day.

"Your car is locked, so I just left the box on your trunk." He hurried by me like he was late for something.

"Thank you," I called after him. I looked at Davida, who was busy texting. Noticing my eyes on her, she looked up. "I'm going to head out. I need to try to find my Airbnb before it gets dark."

She gave a curt nod. "See you tomorrow then."

Walking through the house, I noticed how much we had done. I even entertained the idea that we could be ahead of schedule. Maybe things were looking up after all.

Chapter 9

My Airbnb wasn't too far from the Valley Inn. It took longer to find than it should have, but I was pleasantly surprised once I pulled into the driveway. The quaint cottage was even cuter in real life than in pictures. It was genuinely tiny, smaller than any house I'd ever seen. Nestled back in the woods, it was covered with wooden shingled siding painted a cool lavender that offset it from the surrounding green foliage. A gray cobblestone walkway meandered up to the front door. I was so glad to be away from the Valley Inn and Mr. Xavier that I could feel my muscles relaxing as I got out of the car.

The front door led directly into a small living room. Thick beige carpet padded my footsteps. A light blue slip-covered sofa sat against one wall. The white lace curtains were open, letting the last bit of sunlight filter in, casting a golden glow around the room. I took a deep breath, inhaling the light floral scent in the air. So far, this looked like it would be a good place to stay. Once I got all my belongings situated, I showered, ordered some takeout, and settled in for the night.

Freshly showered and comfortably full, I sat on the floor in the living room with the box of newspapers. I put the latest *Law and Order SVU* episode on to keep me company while I looked through the box I brought from the manor. I wanted to see if it contained the same thing as the one I'd previously looked through. When I opened the flaps, a yellowed newspaper looked up at me. Leaning in, I read the date on top, August 7, 1938. I lifted the newspaper from the box and unfolded it. Pieces of brittle paper flaked off onto the floor as I gingerly straightened the pages.

"Where are you, Raoul?" I scanned the pages for his face. It didn't take long to find him. His photo was on the bottom left corner of the fifth page. He stood scowling out at me. His normally serene face was creased with displeasure as he stared into the camera. This picture wasn't like the others. Raoul wasn't alone. A tall, thin woman stood next to him. Her long skirt looked heavy on her narrow frame. She looked down, the brim of her hat obscuring her face. She stood with one hand folded across her waist and the other reaching up to touch her collarbone. Most of her weight leaned onto her left foot, and I couldn't tell from the picture whether she was a light-skinned black woman or a white woman. Since she was photographed standing with Raoul at this particular moment in history, I naturally assumed she was black. I leaned over to get a closer look at the picture. Something about her was familiar. I reached down and touched the picture. The paper was smooth beneath my skin. When I lifted my hand away, I swore I saw Raoul wink at me. I jumped back.

I was just tired. I'd been working so hard, and so many weird things had been going on that my mind was playing tricks on me. I folded the newspaper and stuck it back in the box. There was no need to go through any more of those newspapers now. If I kept this up, I would drive myself crazy before this project was over.

Settling onto the sofa, I found a romantic comedy to watch, something predictable and comforting that would make me feel good inside. A bit of fluff was the perfect distraction.

****

I woke with a start, wondering where I was at first. Darkness blanketed the room. I sat up in bed, blinking rapidly, trying to focus on what was around me. A sliver of light streamed in through the crack in the curtain from the cabin's porch light. The sheets were wrapped around my legs. I had the distinct feeling I wasn't alone.

"Who's there?" I spoke into the darkness, my voice hoarse with sleep. I swore someone had been standing over me as I slept, or was it only a dream? I untangled my legs from the sheets and swung them over the edge of the bed. Part of me was afraid someone might reach out from underneath and grab me. I could make out silhouettes of the objects in the room, all unfamiliar. In the corner by the closet sat a wicker chair. I reached up and turned on the lamp on the bedside table. A halo of yellow light chased away the darkness. There was no one there with me. The chair across from the bed was empty, except for my suitcase sitting on it. Everything was as it should have been. Still, it didn't feel right. My mouth felt cottony, so I decided to get a glass of water. I padded across the carpet from the bedroom to the living room, turning on lights as I went. Even though I knew the light would steal away even more of my sleepiness, I was too unsure about the house to walk around in the dark, and part of me still expected to find something sinister lurking somewhere. The living room was just as it should've been, unchanged from when I went to bed. I was opening the bottled water I had stored in the fridge when I noticed a newspaper on the kitchen table. I knew I had not put it there.

I put the bottle down on the kitchen table. "Who's here?" I yelled. I tore through the house, opening closets and looking under furniture.

As I yanked open closet doors and knelt to look under the bed, I knew what I was doing was foolish. If someone was hiding in the house, what would I do when I found them? What kind of person would hide in a cottage and move things around just to mess with my head? The whole thing was insane. I was acting irrationally. We've all had those moments. This was one of those moments for me. Once I was certain I had searched through every inch of the house and checked every window and door, I returned to the kitchen. I don't know if it was because fear heightened my senses or what, but as I stepped back into the kitchen, the tile floor seemed extra cold and hard against the soles of my bare feet.

The air around me seemed to be charged with electricity, prickling my skin and making the hair on my arms stand on end. I approached the kitchen table. That newspaper must have been put there for a reason, and even though I didn't like this game, I wanted to understand it. Cautiously, I approached it like I thought the paper would jump up from the table and attack me. Not touching it, I leaned over, looking at the small print on the yellowing page. I knew what I was looking for but didn't find it. Another photo caught my eye. It was bigger than the rest. A shadowy figure stood on a hill. The details of the figure were impossible to make out, but they felt familiar to me. I stared at the photo, holding it under the light. I felt like I should know this picture, this place, this person, but how?

CHAPTER 10

E xhausted from yet another restless night, I drove to Warner Manor. I had no intention of going inside alone, so I decided to sit in my car and wait for someone else to arrive. I texted the owner of my Airbnb to ask if anyone else had the key. When I told him I thought someone else had been in the cottage while I slept, he responded with the appropriate amount of shock but didn't offer me much comfort. Honestly, I don't think he believed me. I didn't know what I was supposed to do and was too tired to deal with that right then.

I must've drifted off in my car. The next thing I knew, someone was rapping on the glass on the driver's side window. I jumped. Disoriented at first, I looked over to see Davida through the window.

"Good morning," she said. "You're here bright and early."

"I don't know about the bright part. My head is killing me. I didn't get much sleep last night."

She cocked her head at me. "What happened?"

"I swear someone was in the cottage. When I got up in the middle of the night, a newspaper was spread out across the table, and I didn't put it there." My voice shook a little as I talked.

Davida grimaced. "Did you call the owner?"

"I texted him. He wasn't much help."

"That's because it was probably him. That's why I don't stay in Airbnbs. Any creep can own one."

"You're not making me feel any better."

"I'm not trying to make you feel better. I'm trying to be realistic." She looked into my eyes for a moment, her face softening. "You look terrible. You obviously need to get some sleep."

"I'll be fine. If I get too tired, I'll go back to the Airbnb and lay down for a bit." I knew good and well that I didn't want to go back to that Airbnb, but I didn't have much of a choice.

"Or you could book a hotel room."

My back ached as I got out of the car. The house looked less like my dream these days and more like a nightmare. As I scanned the front of the house, I noticed the door stood wide open. "Have you been inside already?"

"No. I thought you had." She looked over at the house.

We stood next to each other in the driveway, staring at the open door, a sinister invitation beckoning us inside. "Maybe you forgot to shut it last night." It was something that could happen when people got busy. I left early, so I didn't know what had happened once I was gone.

Davida shook her head. "I distinctly remember locking the door. I was talking to JJ and dropped my keys on the ground. We both reached down to get them and bumped heads." She walked toward the front door.

"Maybe we shouldn't go in by ourselves, just in case someone's in there," I called after her, knowing that my suggestion was useless. Davida was more stubborn than I was.

She turned around and looked at me as she approached the door. "I'm in charge here, so it's my responsibility." Then she disappeared inside.

Not wanting to let Davida face whoever was in there alone, I ran after her. "Wait." I nearly stumbled through the door, bumping into her. She stood just inside the entrance in the spot where the chandelier had nearly fallen on her before.

"What is all of this?" She looked at the wall next to the staircase with her mouth agape.

All the muscles in my body tensed, fear gathering at the base of my throat as I turned to see what she saw. Scrawled on the wall and dripping red paint read the words, "Khadijah, I've been waiting for you." And all around, the number eight was written again and again.

"I don't like this. I don't like this at all." Davida shook her head as she spoke. She looked at me. "This is no good. You have to go. You have to go back to the city right now, today." She pushed me out the door. "It's dangerous for you to be here."

I left willingly. I didn't want to stay in there looking at that either. "But what about the house?"

Davida stopped and put her hand on her hip. She motioned back toward the wall. "Look at that. Some maniac is writing your name on the walls, and you're asking me, what about the house? What about you?"

I knew what she meant. I was feeling the same way.

"We need to sell this place and get out of here." Davida came out onto the porch with me.

"I don't think we can sell it. Nobody wanted to touch it before I bought it." I watched the door, aware we hadn't checked to ensure no one was still in there. What if someone came running out now and attacked us?

Just then, JJ pulled into the circular driveway.

He got out with a smile on his face. "It's a beautiful morning." His smile disappeared as he walked toward us. He looked from Davida to me before asking, "What's going on?"

"Look inside." Davida motioned toward the front door. I stepped aside so he could get through.

He walked inside, but the graffiti didn't seem to scare him like it did me. "Squatters got in again. They must've broken the window somewhere." He started to walk through the foyer to the living room. I called out to him.

"Don't you think it's strange that squatters would know my name?" I went back inside to get another look at the graffiti.

He stopped and turned to look at it again. "I guess."

"I think something a little more sinister is going on here than just squatters," Davida said.

"Do you think someone in town is trying to scare you away?" JJ asked.

I thought for a minute. His suggestion made sense, more sense than what I was initially thinking. I'd jumped to a supernatural explanation, mostly because my imagination tended to get a bit out of control. "JJ's got a point. It could be someone trying to scare me off. It is public record that I'm the owner of this place. Anyone searching for the information could find my name." I like how rational I sounded. That was much better than how I had been feeling.

"I don't care if it's a squatter or someone from town. I don't like how menacing it looks. What if someone tries to do something to

Khadijah?" The creases on Davida's forehead deepened as she looked at the graffiti. "I can't in good conscience stand by and let her be threatened like this and pretend nothing is happening. We don't know when whoever is doing this is going to stop writing threats and start taking action."

"Where's the threat?" JJ asked, motioning to the writing on the wall. "I see a bunch of numbers and a welcome message." He looked at me. "Welcome home? Have you been here before?"

I shook my head. "I don't know what that's all about." The first time I laid eyes on this place in person was the day I came to get the keys from Alton. I pulled my phone out again. "I'm going to call the police officer that was here before and have him come look around. We should do that before we go inside."

JJ was already walking further into the house. "You don't think I can handle myself," he said as he walked away from me.

I was already on the phone with the police when JJ went upstairs to see what was on the second floor. "Davida, Khadijah, come here. You won't believe this," he called.

Davida raised her eyebrows at me before cautiously starting up the stairs. I stayed put until I'd finished my call. When I hung up, she was already at the top of the stairs.

"Are you coming up?"

I didn't want to, but I felt like I should. Anyway, I didn't want to stay downstairs by myself either. "Officer Moses will be here in a few minutes. We could just wait until he gets here." I was already at the top of the stairs when I said this.

"I want to see what JJ found." She walked up the hallway. "JJ, where are you?"

"Back here." He stepped into the corridor from the farthest room.

The walls upstairs were covered in eights, just like downstairs. I wondered how many people did this and why.

"What's with the number eight?" Davida asked.

"I have no idea." I stopped, overwhelmed by the amount of work it must've taken. Did they paint the entire house this way?

"This is probably the work of teenagers. It's the kind of thing they would get up to." I figured Davida would know since she had teenagers of her own.

"Are you guys coming?" JJ's voice came up the hall.

I shuddered to think what might be in that room, but I couldn't run away from it either. This was my house. If something bad was happening inside of it, that was my responsibility. So even though witnessing whatever JJ wanted me to see was the last thing I wanted, I went to the room.

I stood to the side of the doorway, so inside the room was out of my field of vision, and watched Davida look inside. Her mouth fell open.

"What in the devil is that?" She stepped inside the room, a look of confusion on her face.

Since she didn't scream in horror, I knew it was nothing terrible, so I took a deep breath and stepped through the doorway.

CHAPTER 11

The metallic scent of blood met me as I stepped through the doorway. In the center of the room stood what I could only describe as an effigy. It was in the crude shape of a person, with each body part fashioned from a bundle of sticks. Dark blood stained the torso of the stick man.

"Jesus." I covered my nose with my index finger, immediately put off by the smell. Two dead cats lay at the effigy's feet—their heads missing. Their soft bellies had been torn open, and their glistening innards unspooled. I stared at their small, lifeless bodies. Something about them repulsed me and drew me in all at once.

"What is this?" Davida turned and looked at me as if I knew the answer.

I shook my head. "This is sick. That's what it is."

"This is some voodoo stuff here. I wonder how long it took them to do all this?" JJ seemed more in awe than disgusted.

Just then, I heard someone walking around downstairs. "Hello?" I recognized Officer Moses's deep, resonant voice.

With my arms crossed over my chest, hugging myself, I walked toward the staircase. "We're up here." I listened and heard his footsteps coming up the stairs. He wasn't alone. Officer Moses and Alton appeared at the top of the staircase.

"We were having breakfast together when you called. I hope you don't mind," Alton said.

"We already saw the graffiti downstairs." Officer Moses walked past me to the back room. "Did they do any other damage? Back here?" He pointed. He could already see Davida standing in the doorway.

"Yeah, you should get a look at this," Davida said.

Officer Moses stepped into the room.

"Are you all right?" Alton asked.

I nodded. "Just a little shaken up, that's all."

"It's going to be okay." He said it like he knew something I didn't.

I smiled tightly as if his words were reassuring. I followed Officer Moses into the room.

We all stood gaping up at the effigy.

"You have to admit, it's pretty impressive," JJ said.

The crude statue was so tall that it touched the ceiling.

"Why do they have to keep killing cats?" Davida shook her head.

Alton walked around the effigy, examining it. "This is a spell." He looked at me. "Someone is trying to hex you."

"Hex? What do you mean by hex?" Davida asked.

He continued walking around the stick man, leaning close to it, trying to take in every detail. "What's this?" He pointed to the chest, where there was a smear of dark blood.

"I think it's blood." JJ stood next to him, looking at it.

"Not that. There's something inside it." He reached forward, grabbed hold of something, and pulled it out of the bundle of sticks that made up the torso.

"Don't touch anything," Officer Moses said, but it was too late because Alton had already pulled out what looked like a piece of string. It dangled between his fingers.

"Is that your necklace?" Davida asked.

Reflexively, I brought my hand up to my throat. I went over to Alton, bending down to get a closer look. My blood chilled as soon as I saw the small, hammered medallion with my initials on its face. "I lost that right before I came up here." The day before I came, my necklace had disappeared. I thought it was so strange because I remembered taking it off and leaving it on my nightstand before I went to bed like I always did, but when I got up in the morning, I couldn't find it anywhere. I'd searched the bedroom, and it was nowhere to be found. Eventually, I decided to leave, knowing it would turn up once I got home. I didn't expect it to turn up here. "I don't understand. How did it get here?"

My legs could no longer support me. As I melted to the floor, Alton and JJ caught my arms, lifting me. "I need to lay down for a minute."

Everyone started moving around quickly. I heard Davida say something about taking me to her truck, and before I knew it, I was lifted off the ground by someone. My mind was swimming. The numbers, the effigy, my necklace—I couldn't understand how these things were connected.

I was in a haze. Then I felt the sun on my face, and I was sitting in the cab of Davida's truck. The warm sunlight shone on me through the windshield. The door stood open, letting the cold air drift in. Davida stood next to me, her hand on my shoulder. She was talking, but not to me. Alton stood next to her.

"When you say this is a hex, what exactly do you mean?" she asked him.

I was able to get out of my thoughts enough to listen and understand.

"Just what I said. Someone is casting a spell on Khadijah."

The sound of my name made me sit up straighter in my seat. I couldn't afford to be slumped over. I needed to pay attention if I wanted to fight whatever was happening. "But who would do this?" My voice was so soft it was barely there.

Alton shifted uncomfortably on his feet before speaking. "Well, do you have any enemies?"

I had gone through my entire life trying my best to make friends everywhere. I found that if I was likable enough, I could get what I wanted. I wasn't the type of person who had enemies. "I don't even know anyone here."

Alton looked at the house and then back at me. "I can't imagine anyone being so angry that you bought this property that they would go through the trouble of casting such a complicated spell." He was deep in thought, looking at his shoes. Davida and I looked at him, waiting to see what he might say next.

When we were tired of waiting, Davida finally spoke. "I don't believe any of this nonsense. Don't come here talking about people casting spells and curses; we have enough to worry about. Someone is mad because we bought this house, and now, they're trying to scare us off. We don't get scared that easily." She made eye contact with me. Then she turned her attention back to Alton. "You suggesting some kind of magic is going on here is not helping anything."

Alton opened his mouth to speak again, but Davida held up her hand.

"If you're about to say anything else about curses and spells, don't bother."

"Look," Alton said. "I'm not trying to cause a problem here. I'm only telling you what's going on. There were all kinds of rumors going around about what you're going to do with this place. I wouldn't be surprised if someone has it out for you."

"Someone's definitely messing with me." I found a bit more strength in my voice now. "The graffiti on the walls, the number eight written on my car windows, and last night someone broke into my Airbnb and spread out one of the newspapers I brought home on the table."

"What newspaper?" Alton asked.

Davida answered his question. "There are boxes of old newspapers in the house. We think it's an art project Raoul was working on because they all have pictures of him inside."

Alton gave her a questioning look but didn't pursue the topic. "My grandmother is a root worker. I can have her come around to take a look at things," he paused, "if you decide to stick around." He shrugged a little.

"We'll definitely be sticking around." Davida spoke forcefully. Then she angled her gaze at me, and her face softened. "I will, at least. Khadijah should probably head back to the city for a little bit."

Only a few minutes before, I would've agreed with her. I was thinking the exact same thing when I walked into the house and saw all the graffiti on the walls. Now I was having second thoughts. I didn't want to run away. Someone was obviously trying to scare me. I wasn't sure why, but I knew I didn't want them to win. "I'll stick around for a while. I was originally planning to be here for a month. I should stick it out."

"There's really no reason for you to be here," Davida reiterated.

"Stop saying that. You make me feel useless."

"Nobody's saying that. I'm used to doing this without you. Under the circumstances, it's perfectly reasonable for you not to be here."

"Perfectly reasonable," I muttered. Was anything perfectly reasonable anymore?

Officer Moses came out of the house and walked over to the truck. "I found another window broken in the back of the house. That's probably where they got in. JJ is boarding it up now. There's not much I can do to keep them out. And right now, I have no idea who's doing it." He spoke slowly, dragging out as words as if doing so somehow made what he had to say easier to digest. "We don't have the resources to stake out an empty construction project."

"We don't expect you to," Davida said quickly.

"It's probably just teenagers playing a prank." Officer Moses looked at the house.

"I know a lot about this stuff. It's no prank." Alton spoke quickly. "My grandmother can fix this. I know it."

"If that's something you believe in." Officer Moses looked at Alton and then back at me. "Getting her advice wouldn't hurt."

Davida shook her head. "We don't need anything like that." She looked at me and was surprised to see the expression on my face.

"Maybe we do," I whispered.

CHAPTER 12

Alton's grandmother showed up later that afternoon in a sputtering station wagon that was so dented and rusty I couldn't say what color it was originally. The car coughed out a cloud of black smoke as it lurched to a stop in the driveway.

I walked over to the car as she swung the door open and got out. She was a small, sturdy woman with skin like red clay. A navy blue felt fedora was smashed down onto her head, pushing the tops of her ears out. A thin cigarette hung from her mouth. She dropped it to the ground and squished it into the gravel beneath her pointed turquoise cowboy boot. "Are you Khadijah?" Her voice was deeper than I expected.

I reached out to shake her hand. "Yes, I am. You're Alton's grandmother?"

She took my hand in a firm grip. "You can call me Glory. My grandson says somebody's hexing you."

"That's what he told me. I don't know how true it is. I mean, I don't really—" I stopped myself before finishing the sentence, but she did it for me.

"—believe in this stuff."

Part of me wanted to shrink from her. "I guess not, but I thought having you look around wouldn't hurt."

She tutted at me, shaking her head. "It's always the ones that really need to believe that don't." She put her hands on her hips and looked up at the house. "You got yourself into a mighty fine mess buying this house, haven't you?" She walked past me up the porch steps. When she got to the front door, she turned to see me gaping at her. "Aren't you going to show me inside?"

"Yeah, of course." I hurried up the stairs feeling a bit discombobulated. There was something about her that made me doubt everything. It was like she could see into me, and I was terrified of what she might discover. She stopped in the entryway where the number eight was written again and again on the wall all around. She stepped forward and touched one of the numbers on the wall. "How long has this been here?"

"Someone did it last night when they did the stuff upstairs." I nodded toward the steps.

She pressed her lips into a thin line and nodded her head. "Let's go upstairs."

The air settled around her as he moved confidently through the house. Everything went silent except for the sound of her footsteps as she walked casually up the stairs.

I hurried behind her, my heart in my throat.

"Why would someone want to hex you?" She walked up the second-floor hallway like she knew exactly where she was going.

"I don't know."

She stopped and turned to face me. "You must know something." She looked at me for a good long time before turning and looking up the hallway. "Where are we going?"

"It's the last room up here on the right." I walked in front of her. Stopping short of the room, I motioned to it with my hand. The last thing I wanted to do was set foot in there again.

She took a few deep breaths, her shoulders going up and down exaggeratedly. "There's definitely something rotting in here."

I stood just beyond the doorway, watching her for a moment before stepping forward to look into the room myself. JJ had taken the dead cats away, but the scent of rotting flesh lingered. I held my arm over my nose to cover up the sickly odor.

She took long, steady strides around the room, circling the effigy at its center. Then she stopped and pulled her reading glasses from the pocket of her denim shirt. Slipping them on, she leaned in, looking closely at the effigy. "There's something in here." She reached out and pulled some of the sticks and straw away that made up its torso.

"What?" I fought my instincts and stepped closer.

A bit of pink flesh peeked through the sticks. With some force, she pulled more away. The effigy wobbled, and I reached out to steady it. Finally, she revealed what looked to be a piece of raw meat with twine wrapped in a crisscross pattern around it.

"Do you know what that is?" She looked at me with a spark of mischief in her eyes.

I shook my head.

"It's a pig heart. Someone's doing some serious working on you." She put her hands on her hips and stared into the cavity she'd cleared in the effigy. "Whoever did this knows what they're doing." She looked around at the walls.

Panic surged through me. Did that mean that she couldn't help? If she couldn't help me, what was I supposed to do? "My necklace was in it too."

Glory nodded knowingly. "Whatever they're fixing to do here is going to be strong." She looked at me, her eyes narrow. "Was there anything else here, like a sacrifice perhaps?"

I wondered how she knew. I had completely forgotten to tell her. "Yes. There were two dead cats. We found more cats on another day too."

She didn't look surprised. "Someone is trying to bind your heart to something or someone."

"What does that mean?"

She pressed her lips together, puckering them about before answering. "It could mean any number of things. Only the person who cast the spell really knows. I can take an educated guess at what the intention is."

"And?" I asked.

"I'm not sure yet, but I will figure it out in time." She walked around the effigy again, taking the details in with her eyes.

"I need this to stop as soon as possible." The only reason I called her was because Alton had implied that she could do something to help. "I can't keep doing this. It's messing with my head."

She looked at me over her glasses, her gaze cutting. "Something else happened, something besides this." She gestured toward the effigy.

"So much has happened since I've gotten here. I don't know where to start. One night, I was here alone, and someone else was in here with me, a squatter probably. That's what I thought at the time, but now I wonder. Maybe they were here to do something else. I was staying at the Valley Inn, and some strange stuff has happened there too."

At the mention of my bed and breakfast, she frowned. "Gladys is a good woman, but Douglas—" She shook her head. "He likes to stick his nose in where it doesn't belong."

I immediately recalled how creepy all my interactions with him had been. "He gave me a bad feeling. Anyway, when I was staying there, I was in the shower, and someone wrote the number eight over and over in the steam on the mirror."

"Like downstairs on the walls?"

"Exactly like that."

She nodded firmly. "They've been hexing you for a while."

I heard footsteps coming up the hall. Davida appeared in the doorway. "It stinks in here." She crinkled her face.

"There's a pig's heart in there." I pointed at the effigy.

Davida drew her head back and looked at the effigy. "That's messed up. So, what does it all mean?" She stood with her arms crossed and her feet firmly planted.

Instead of addressing Davida, Glory spoke directly to me. "I'll prepare some candles for protection and a mojo bag. It will help. Since you're friends with my grandson, I won't charge you this time."

Davida raised an eyebrow. I hoped she wouldn't say anything.

"Thank you. I really appreciate that." I anticipated getting a lecture from Davida about how foolish this was. "The candles and the bag will protect me, and I can stay here and finish working, right?"

I looked at Davida, who let out a harrumph, making her disapproval known. "It doesn't matter how many candles and mojo bags you have. You should still go home."

Glory ignored her yet again. "Yes. The things I'll give you will keep you safe. You won't have to worry. Still, you must catch whoever is doing it and stop them. Whenever they do a new spell or try to strengthen this one, I'll give you something else to counteract it. Then we'll work on turning the hex back on them tenfold." Glory walked over to the door.

Davida stepped aside without her asking.

"I'll prepare everything and bring them back to you in a week," she said over her shoulder, already walking up the hall.

"That's a long time," I said.

"I'm a busy woman. I'm doing something for you for free. It will take as long as it takes. If you want it done right, it'll take a week." She was firm.

I hurried out after her. "Can I get rid of all of this stuff?"

"It's best to burn it. Burn it and bury the ashes." Her voice croaked as she spoke.

"Where?" I asked.

She stopped as if thinking. Then she gave a little shrug. "That's for you to figure out."

I hated that answer.

"Take all of it outside, make a big fire, and bury the ashes." She thought for a moment. "I'll prepare some railroad spikes to protect the property. I'll cleanse this whole place and surround it with protection."

I nodded as if I understood what any of this meant. She paused, looking into my eyes for a while. Her tough exterior cracked for a moment, and she reached up and touched my cheek. "You've got some powerful magic working against you, but you don't have to worry. I'm right here. Any friend of Alton's is a friend of mine. I take good care of my friends."

"Thank you." She turned to walk away again, and then I remembered something. "Do you know anything about Raoul Bonnaire?"

She turned again to face me. "This is his house."

"Yes. That's why I bought it. But I figure you were probably around back then. Am I right to assume that?"

She nodded.

"Was there anything unusual about him?"

A sly grin slid across her face. "Everything about Raoul was unusual."

"You knew him, then?"

"You could say that." She walked back up the hallway closer to me. "He was more than an artist."

"What do you mean?"

"I used to clean this house when he lived here. He wasn't just making art here." Her eyes clouded with memory, and she seemed to be looking past me at something else.

Curious, I turned around to look behind me but saw nothing interesting.

"What else was he doing?"

"I don't know exactly. He was secretive." She drew the corners of her mouth down. I could tell she was lost in her memories. "There was a room he'd spend a lot of time in downstairs that I wasn't allowed to clean. It was always locked, but one day I tried to get in. He caught me and was so mad that he fired me on the spot. It was too bad because this was the best cleaning job in town."

"I have some newspapers. There are boxes of them from different years, and they all contain pictures of him. Was he working on something involving that?"

Glory shook her head. "He didn't want me to know anything about his work."

"Do you have any theories about him?"

"Theories?" Glory asked. She thought for a moment. "There are stories in this town. I've heard them all."

"Mr. Xavier told me some things about this house."

"You heard about John?" Glory asked me.

I nodded.

"You know then. There are immortals among us. I wouldn't be surprised if Raoul was one."

"Give me a break." I'd forgotten Davida was behind me.

Glory scowled. "You don't have to believe something for it to be true. Some things are true whether or not you believe."

"There's no such thing as people who live forever." Davida wagged her finger at me. "Don't get caught up in these silly stories."

I appreciated that Davida wanted to protect me, but I didn't need her protection. I needed answers. "I want to hear what she has to say." I held up my hand to her. "What are immortals?"

"Every culture has its stories. I've come to realize that some of those stories are true." With that, she turned around and walked down the stairs like she had nothing more to share with us, but I had more questions now than ever before.

CHAPTER 13

O range flames licked the air as the effigy burned.

"I can't believe we're actually doing this." Davida stood next to me, watching the flames rise in the air and drinking her third cup of coffee of the day. Dark smoke billowed skyward.

The whole crew took a break to watch the spectacle.

"Do you feel better now?" Davida looked at me.

I thought for a moment. "Yes, actually I do."

Davida gave a gentle nod. "I'm glad, but that doesn't mean you're out of harm's way. I still think you should head home." She was only trying to do what was best for me, and I did appreciate that.

"I think I'll stick around." The situation at my Airbnb tugged at my thoughts. I didn't really want to go back there. So far, I hadn't stayed anywhere I felt safe.

We watched the fire until the flames died, leaving smoldering ash behind. Everyone went back to work except me. I stood in the field looking at the pile of ash. I needed to bury it, and to do that, I needed a hole.

The shovel sliced through the grass, exposing rich dark soil underneath. The weather was just changing to fall, and I appreciated the cool breeze on my skin as I dug. Turning over the dirt made me feel accomplished. As the hole got deeper and my pile of dirt grew, I felt like I had more control over my life. After a while, the muscles in my back strained, and my arms and shoulders began to ache. Several times, people from the crew and even Davida herself came out to talk to me to ask about what I was doing and if they could help. Each time, I turned them down. Digging was my therapy, and I wanted to do it alone. I don't know how long I'd been digging when I found it. My shovel came into contact with something solid. I poked around, trying to determine the size of whatever I was hitting. It wasn't as hard as a rock but softer, more like a tree root. I was far enough from the trees that I shouldn't have been hitting anything. I began excavating the area, scraping away the dirt and searching for the object's edges.

I finally stuck the shovel underneath it, leveraging it to lift the object from the dirt. It broke free, lifting a few inches. When I pulled it out, I found it was a wooden box roughly three feet long, two feet wide, and one foot tall. Clumps of dirt still clung to the splintering wood. Large nails held the sides together. I felt like I was meant to find it. It was as if I'd been drawn to this place to dig. I exhaled and lifted the lid.

"What do you have there?" The voice startled me so badly that I let go of the lid, and it fell closed before I even saw inside. I looked up, squinting into the sun to see Davida standing at the edge of the hole. "I'm really worried about you. I wish you would just go back to the city." She frowned.

I looked at myself, covered in soil, my nails caked in dirt, sweat streaming down my face, and I knew what she meant. I was never the superstitious type, but here I was, following the instructions of a root worker. "I know what this looks like, but I swear everything's fine." I pointed at the box like she hadn't just asked me about it. "Look what I found."

"I see." Davida raised an eyebrow. "What's inside?" She was naturally curious and couldn't help but have a look inside.

"I don't know. Let's find out." I lifted the lid, heavy with moisture after being buried in the ground for so long. A dark mass of something lay crumbled inside.

"What is it?" Her words were impatient. She squatted next to me.

I didn't want to reach inside and touch whatever it was, so I tipped the box so its contents fell out into the dirt. Only as it tumbled out did I realize that the dark lump was fabric. Davida reached out and took hold of it before I could. She held it up, revealing that it was an old-fashioned dress. The fabric was stiff, but the dress seemed to be fully intact. The pleats and gathers didn't fall easily like fabric normally would, and when held up, it remained so bunched it was hard to make out the details. The neckline dipped slightly. The shoulders were full. I stood up next to Davida so I could get a better look at the dress without the sun in my eyes. Upon closer inspection, I saw that it wasn't black but a deep, rich purple.

"That's weird. Who buries a dress?" Davida asked.

Who indeed? I reached out and touched it. The fabric was stiff and rough. As soon as I touched it, something like a memory came into my mind.

I was running in the woods, the ground slick beneath my feet as something chased me. I could hear it breathing behind me, and fear coursed through my veins. I ran faster. Slipping on the leaves, I fell back. The tops of the trees came into view before everything went black and dropped away.

"Khadijah, are you okay?" Davida had put the dress back into the box and was looking at me with her head tilted.

I shook my head, trying to shake myself back into the here and now. "Yeah, I'm fine. I just remembered something." My words slowed. "I don't mean remembered. I don't know what I mean."

"You need some rest." Her voice softened as she closed the box.

I felt dizzy and disoriented. The walls of the hole seemed to come alive around me. I was aware of all of the worms and insects burrowing through the soil. A cacophony of sounds filled my ears. Then the soil started to cave in around me, gathering around my feet. I yelped and turned, trying to crawl out of the hole that suddenly seemed much deeper than I had dug it. Each time I reached for the dirt to pull myself up, it gave way, sending me tumbling back down into the hole again. Worms slithered around me, dirt sticking to their slimy bodies. Then the worms seemed to morph into fingers before my eyes. Hands shot up from the earth, grasping at me. The fingernails scraped my flesh. I yelled and struck the hands away, trying to pull them off me. Tears streamed down my face as I imagined myself being pulled underground, buried alive.

"Khadijah! Khadijah, calm down! Stop it! I'm trying to help you."

The hands I was hitting away were Davida's.

"What is going on with you?" she asked.

With that question, I seemed to crumble. I fell into her, sobbing.

"It's going to be okay." She rubbed my back.

She took me by the arm and helped me climb clumsily out of the hole. "I don't understand what happened. It was like suddenly I was in a deep hole by myself, and it was all filling in on me." I was still out of breath as I talked. Davida led me across the field to the driveway to sit in her pickup truck.

"Is everything okay out here?" JJ walked over to the truck. "I thought I heard Khadijah screaming." He looked at me with concern in his eyes.

"Everything's fine." Davida had an authority to her voice that you couldn't help but believe.

JJ gave me one last look. "Well, if you need anything, you know where I am." He turned and walked back to the house, where some other workers were standing on the porch watching us.

Davida stepped away from the truck. "Go back to work. Everything's fine here. Khadijah just isn't feeling very well."

With that, everyone went back inside. Davida stood next to her truck, her feet wide and her hands on her hips, watching until they all got inside. Once they were gone, she turned her attention back to me. I sat on the edge of the passenger seat with my legs dangling outside of the truck. "I really think you shouldn't be here anymore."

I nodded slightly.

Davida continued, "You need to go home."

I nodded again. My mind was still reeling from whatever had happened to me. There was no real reason to be here besides to see the house of an artist I admired. I'd done that. I could go home.

I looked across the field. "I haven't buried that yet." I pointed weakly at the ashes. "That's why I was digging the hole."

Davida let out an exasperated sigh. "I know. I'll bury it for you. Don't worry about it."

"Okay," I whispered.

Davida was reluctant to let me drive back to the Airbnb on my own. It took some convincing for her to finally let me go. As I drove, I ran over the events of the afternoon in my head. So much had happened that I felt like a week had passed, but it had only been one day. Now, here I was, going back to the Airbnb that had scared me so much the night before. I was so tired all I wanted to do was lie down and take a nap, but I wasn't going to be able to do it there.

I went inside to gather up what little I had left there. As soon as I opened the door, the pungent odor of raw sewage hit me. I heard the sound of water splashing. I ran to the bathroom to see sludge bubbling up out of the toilet and oozing out onto the floor. I gagged, covering my nose and mouth with my hand to block out the smell. It was disgusting, revolting, so much so that I decided right then and there to abandon my toiletries. I could buy a new toothbrush. I pulled the door closed and immediately called the owner. I put my things back in my suitcase and put them in the car. When I grabbed the box of newspapers, I noticed it was open. I peered inside, and a different paper was on the top of the box than before. It was the one with the pictures of Raoul and a woman. The photo was on top of the pile, staring back at me. The woman looked down, so I couldn't see her face clearly, but I recognized her dress. I pulled the paper out of the box and spread it out on the hood of my car, looking at it more closely. I was no clothing expert, but it definitely could've been the same dress I'd found in the hole. Why was the dress buried in the ground? Who was this woman? Why did she feel so familiar to me?

CHAPTER 14

I never thought I'd end up back at the Valley Inn, but the owner of the Airbnb was so distressed by the plumbing situation that he got me a room there. Apparently, he was good friends with the Xaviers. Part of me knew I should just go home like Davida suggested, but I was so tired that I couldn't imagine driving that far. I sighed as I pulled into the parking lot. I hadn't cleaned up at all and still had streaks of dirt on my face and caked beneath my nails as I pulled my suitcase out of the car. Mr. Xavier came out onto the porch as if he had been watching through the front window, waiting for my arrival.

He crossed his arms over his chest and gave me a once-over. "What happened to you?"

"I'm renovating a house."

He nodded. "I didn't think you would do any physical labor."

"Usually, I don't, but this job is personal." I stood next to my suitcase, hoping he'd offer to help me with it, but of course, he didn't.

"That's right. I forgot."

I hauled my suitcase up the front porch stairs. Mr. Xavier stepped to the side. "We've got a room for you on the first floor today, so you don't have to lug that up any more stairs." He held the door open for me.

The living room was empty, and the whole place was unusually quiet. "Has it been slow today?"

He pressed his lips together and shrugged. "No slower than usual."

"Usually, people are hanging out here." I nodded toward the couch.

"It's dinner time. They're all out eating somewhere." I followed him up the narrow, carpeted hallway off the living room.

The door to my room already stood open, the last one on the left. "Gladys made sure to fix this one up nice for you." He made a grand sweeping gesture with his arm into the room. "So, there shouldn't be any complaints."

I was too tired to say anything about his smart remark. I just wanted to shower and lie down. I hoped I'd be able to do that safely. I dragged my feet as I maneuvered my suitcase into the room. He handed me a key before pulling the door closed. I listened to the floor creak as he walked away. Once I was sure that he had gone up the hallway, I started the shower. I needed to clean up and get some sleep. Getting some rest would help me think a bit clearer.

I didn't expect sleep to come as easily as it did, but as soon as my head hit the pillow, I was pulled into the world of dreams. At least, I think it was a dream, even though it felt more like a memory. In it, I walked through a field. The grass, wet with dew, brushed the hem of my long skirt. My feet ached from being squeezed into stiff, uncomfortable shoes. My heart raced with fear, but I didn't run. I walked, checking over my shoulder every few steps. There was no one there, just the expansive grass meeting the horizon, but that did nothing to calm me. I reached down, hiking up my skirt so I could move faster. When I looked down, I noticed what I was wearing. Navy ribbon trimmed the hem of the dark purple skirt. Crisscross stitching held the ribbon in place. The shock of the familiarity of the garment stopped me in my tracks. Then I heard a noise behind me, possibly the sharp intake of breath before something heavy struck me on the head.

I sat up in bed with a start. The curtains stood open, and only a hint of dusty light came in the window. My heart thumped wildly in my chest. "It was only a dream," I said to myself. The words rang hollow because it felt like more than a dream. In the dim light, I saw the silhouette of something in the chair on the other side of the room that didn't belong. I swore the chair had been empty when I went to sleep. Switching on the overhead light, I saw the dress I found buried by the house--the dress I wore in the dream. But Davida had returned it to its box. I'd watched her do it. I'd left it at Warner Manor with her.

My heart sunk into my stomach, opening up a hollow feeling in my chest. I rushed to the door, checking it. It was still locked. How could this dress have gotten here? I extended my hand and felt the rough fabric. As I did, the memory of the dream shot into me. The dream in which I was wearing this very dress. Fear roiling through me, I picked it up and balled the rough fabric up. I stuffed it into the closet on the top shelf where I wouldn't have to look at it.

Even with the dress locked in the closet, I still didn't feel safe. How could a dress seem so threatening? I sat down on the bed and tried to put my thoughts together.

I'd worked so hard to be successful and thought that would make me safe. I never had anyone else to depend on. I always had to be self-sufficient, but I couldn't protect myself from everything. I didn't know exactly what was happening, but I knew in my gut that this was more than a prank. The feeling of hopelessness that washed over me made the tears start. With all that was going on, a good cry was exactly what I needed. I had to take a moment to acknowledge my fear.

I was sitting on the bed crying when I swore I saw someone moving outside my window. I hadn't shut the blinds before lying down. And now, someone moved close to the glass in the darkness just beyond the reflection. I jumped to my feet, rushing to the window to look out, but I could only see my own reflection in the glass. I flipped off the light and returned to the window to look out again. There was nothing out there but trees. I pulled the curtain closed and turned the light back on. Was I losing my mind?

I couldn't go back to sleep without finding out, so I marched over to the door, unlocked it, and stepped out into the hallway. I crept up the hallway on bare feet. In front of one of the rooms, I could hear someone softly snoring on the other side of the door. I padded into the living room, which was dark except for a tiny brass lamp with an emerald-green shade on the table behind the sofa.

I walked over to the door and, against my better judgment, stepped out onto the porch. The concrete was ice cold beneath my soles. Goosebumps rose on my exposed skin. I stood on the porch with my arms crossed over my chest, looking over the parking lot. I wasn't alone. Someone else was there, watching me. Just beyond the edge of the parking lot, where the darkness overtook the light of the street-lamps, a dark figure crouched near the bushes.

At that moment, my instincts told me to go back inside and lock the door, but something deeper inside me drove me to do the exact opposite of that. I was tired of being afraid and didn't want to let whoever was out there scare me anymore. They weren't going to win. I took a deep breath and called upon all my courage. Then I marched straight over to where I thought the person was. "Who do you think you are, looking in my window like that?" I admit I wasn't in my right mind. Clearly, what I did was stupid. I was alone in the dark, unarmed, and I decided to approach someone I thought had been threatening me.

No one answered, but I saw movement in the bushes. The figure squatted down even lower like he thought he could hide from me. "I don't know what kind of game you think you're playing, but you need to leave me alone. You don't know who you're messing with." My bark was much bigger than my bite, but the person in the bushes didn't know that.

"What's going on out here?" The voice behind me made me jump out of my skin. I turned to see Mr. Xavier standing on the porch in a blue terry-cloth robe.

I was happy to see him for once. "That guy was peeking in through my window." I pointed at the bushes.

Mr. Xavier came over beside me. He looked to where I pointed. "There's nobody there."

I looked at the patch of mulch between the bushes. "I swear a man was squatting down just over there. He was looking through my window. I saw him."

Mr. Xavier shook his head. "You should come inside. You're going to wake up the other guests."

"You don't understand. There was someone there." I walked into the darkness. It was a moonless night, and I couldn't see very far. No one was there.

Mr. Xavier was shaking his head when he went inside. "Try to stay out of trouble."

I hurried after him through the door, realizing that I wasn't going to accomplish anything standing alone in the dark. Even if I did find the person who was looking through my window, what would I do then? I pulled the door closed behind me.

"How long are you staying here again?" He turned to look at me. "Frank said something about you staying here for a whole month." I heard the disgust in his voice. I was sure he thought he didn't want to deal with me for that long.

"That was my original arrangement for the Airbnb. I assume it'll be functioning again soon, and I'll just go back there. I'll be out of your hair before you know it."

It was ridiculous that he was making a paying customer feel like this. I said good night to Mr. Xavier as cheerily as I could manage.

He replied with a grunt and a wave of the hand before we parted ways in the living room.

When I returned to my room, I still felt uneasy but did my best to settle into bed. Somehow, I managed to get some sleep. My dreams were back to normal, forgettable. I awoke the next morning, ready to start a new day.

CHAPTER 15

I was relieved to see Glory's battered car parked outside Warner Manor when I drove up. I couldn't wait to see what protection she had to offer me. I had gone from someone who didn't believe in any of this to someone who believed in all of it in a matter of days.

I walked over to Glory's car, expecting to see her sitting inside, waiting for someone to show up. She wasn't there. Her keys hung in the ignition. The small alligator's foot attached to her key chain swung back and forth like she had only just gotten out. Squinting into the rising sun, I looked around for her. She stood at the far end of the property where we burned the effigy. The red scarf she wore tied around her head stood out against the green background. I hurried over to her.

"Good morning," I said.

She shook her head and clucked her tongue. "What is this?" She motioned toward the charred remains scattered in the dirt. "I rushed putting together your protections because you were so worried. I moved you to the front of the line—in front of my paying customers—and you didn't even do what I told you to do. How can I help you when you can't follow simple instructions?" She looked up at me. A thin band of gray surrounded her dark irises.

"I know I didn't finish. I ran into some surprises."

She shook her head again. "You always run into surprises when doing the work, but you have to keep going if you want to overcome them. This isn't easy. That's why we call it work. The other side is always throwing surprises at us. That's how they try to win." She motioned to the pile of ashes. "If you leave this uncovered, you're worse off than you were before." She looked around the field, squinting. "Where's your shovel?" Her voice was tense.

I found myself feeling flustered. "In the house."

Her eyes sliced through me. When I didn't move, she said, "Go get it. We'll need two."

While the last thing I wanted to do was start the morning digging, I also knew not to argue. I hurried toward the house, fumbling with my keys and hoping there really were shovels inside. As soon as I opened the door, I found them leaning against the wall next to the staircase. I took them and practically ran back through the field to her.

She continued to frown as I handed her a shovel.

"You shouldn't be doing this. I can do it myself," I said, knowing full well that she wouldn't listen to me.

"I'm a strong old woman. I can dig just as good as anyone." She put the shovel in the ash, now dense with dew, and tipped it into the hole.

My hands were sore from holding the shovel the day before. My back ached. Still, I worked as quickly as I could. Everything was in the hole in no time. Looking down at the unnecessarily deep hole I'd dug filled me with regret. I wanted to stop, but we had to fill it in.

We were still filling in the hole when Davida pulled up. "What's going on here?" She shielded her eyes from the sun as she walked over to us.

Glory stuck her shovel deep into the soil so it stood upright on its own. She wiped her glistening forehead with the sleeve of her shirt. "Someone has to keep you all safe since she didn't seem to care enough about what's going on here to finish what she started." She jabbed her finger in my direction. "You don't understand how serious this is."

Davida glanced at me. "Thank you for finishing this up for us." She spoke slowly as if unsure of each word before it came out of her mouth. "I just worry about you out here digging a hole."

"It's a good thing I'm not digging a hole then. I'm filling it in." Glory took the shovel out of the ground and went back to work. The dirt landed with a thump, and another cloud of dust rose into the air. Davida looked at me.

"Well," she said, "since you two are out here doing this very important work." She looked at me, sarcasm dripping from her words. "I'll get inside and start working on the house." She looked at Glory again, who had heaved a big pile of dirt onto her shovel and stood at the edge of the hole, looking a little bit off-balance. I saw the concern in Davida's eyes. "Can I talk to you inside for a minute?" Davida grabbed my wrist before I could answer and began to pull me toward the house. I dropped my shovel on the ground.

"I'll be right back," I said breathlessly.

"I know you've convinced yourself that something is going on here—"

Before Davida could finish, I cut in. "I haven't convinced myself of anything. Something is going on here. That dress we dug up the other day showed up in my room last night. How did that happen when I left it here with you, unless—" I stopped, a revelation brewing inside me. I looked at Davida with suspicion I hadn't felt before. "Unless you left it there."

She narrowed her eyes at me. "Why would I do something like that?" She looked at the house. "I left it in the house. Did you go in and see if it was still there?"

The idea hadn't even crossed my mind. "Why would I do that? It's in my car right now." When I pulled my key from my pocket, I marched over to my car, opened the trunk, and pulled out the dress. The fabric was stiff. "Here it is."

Davida gazed at the dress for a moment. Then she walked over to me, reached out, and touched the fabric gently, almost as if she was afraid of it. "Are you sure that's the same dress?"

I held it out by the shoulders, letting it unfold. "This is the same dress."

Davida pressed her lips together, thinking. "And you didn't take this back with you."

"Why would I do that? You saw me leave. I didn't take it. You know that."

Davida shook her head. "I don't know what's going on." Davida looked up at me. Her eyes were full of sympathy.

I took a step toward her, dropping the volume of my voice. "Someone was watching me last night. He was looking through my window. When I went outside to check, he was gone."

"Why would someone be watching you?"

"I don't know. How am I supposed to know? I don't understand anything that's going on right now." My voice trembled. I realized I was about to break down.

Davida shook her head.

"I know. I know. You think I should go home." I held up my hand. The last thing I wanted was to go home. I was certain that whatever was going on here would follow me wherever I went.

"I think that woman," Davida nodded toward Glory, "has gotten into your head."

I knew that wasn't true. Everything that was happening in this house was happening before Glory had ever gotten here. "She's only helping."

Davida cocked her head. "Are you sure that's what she's doing?"

I looked through the doorway to the field, where I could see Glory shoveling dirt into the hole. "I'm sure."

I returned to the field to continue helping Glory. I could feel Davida watching me with disapproving eyes as I went.

Sweaty and grimy from filling in the hole, I stepped forward to compact the dirt, when Glory reached out, grabbing hold of my arm, her fingers digging into my flesh. "Leave it. The rain will take care of it tonight."

I was too physically exhausted to even bother asking why. I only nodded weakly. My shoulders ached from two days of digging. Fatigue wrapped around my muscles, and it wasn't even lunchtime yet. I stood, looking at the loose pile of soil. The longer I looked at it, the more my eyes seemed to be playing tricks on me. The soil seemed to move, churning with life. Remembering the hands, I swore grabbed me in the hole yesterday, I stepped back.

"Are you okay, child?" Glory asked.

I looked past her to the dirt, now a normal mound. "Yeah. I just thought I saw something."

She stood, watching me with disapproval in her eyes. After a few minutes, she spoke again. "I'm here because I have something for you." She reached into her pocket and pulled out a red square of fabric tied into a bundle with a piece of twine. "This mojo bag will protect you. I have candles going at my house for you, but I want you to keep this with you." She looked toward the house, which was behind her now. Then she returned her gaze to me. "We'll have to do some workings on the house too. Once the candles are done burning." She gave me a once-over that seemed strangely violating. I felt like I was standing in the middle of the field completely naked. When she was done looking me over, she said, "This isn't a haunting. It's much more than that. Someone is after you." She narrowed her eyes and took a step closer to me. "Someone powerful."

I took the mojo bag from her.

"I made this one extra special just for you." She looked into my eyes as she spoke.

Instinctively I took the bundle of fabric to my nose and took a sniff. The smell was pungent. It smelled of a combination of mint and rich soil.

"You have to keep this with you at all times."

I went to put it into the pocket of my jeans.

She reached for my arm and shook her head. "Put it in your bra so it's close to your heart."

I tucked it into my bra.

Glory nodded with approval. "Good. Don't forget to keep it with you. It's very important." She turned and walked back toward the driveway.

I didn't know whether she was leaving or not. So, I followed her in a daze, my thoughts swirling.

I followed her to the front porch of the house. She turned and looked at me before stepping inside. "I want to go back to the room for a moment if that's okay with you." She raised an eyebrow at me.

I motioned for her to step inside.

We walked straight upstairs past the workman, but it was as if we were alone in the house. I heard nothing and felt nothing. I seemed to float up the stairs.

Before reaching the room, she turned around, stopping so suddenly that I almost walked into her. "I need to go in by myself." Before I could say anything, she walked away from me and disappeared into the room.

I stood in the hallway, my back pressed against the wall, listening. It sounded like Glory was chanting something to herself. Cautiously, I walked to the door and looked in. She stood in the center of the floor with her eyes closed, swaying back and forth. As if realizing I was looking at her, her eyes flew open. "I'll be going now," she announced. She walked past me up the hall.

I followed her closely. "Has this always been something you've done?"

She slowed and turned to look at me before speaking. "I learned from my mother, who had learned from her mother and on down the line. I come from a long line of rootworkers."

"Do you need some kind of special psychic ability to do this?" I didn't even believe in that, but I was curious about what she might say. She approached the top of the stairs.

"We all have some amount of psychic ability. You only need to practice getting in touch with it. I've been practicing ever since I was young, so that makes me better than most at recognizing it, but this is not about being a psychic. It's about knowing how to work with forces you can't see." She grabbed the banister and started down the stairs, lifting her right foot with some effort as she went. "This hex is strong. That means we must do a series of workings to eliminate it." She grimaced at me before stepping outside onto the porch.

It was a crisp fall day. I appreciated how clear and blue the sky was.

"I better get going." She reached out and touched my shoulder. "Be careful. Your working should be done in a few days. Once it is, I will call you and tell you the next steps."

I nodded. "Thank you. I appreciate this so much." I still had no idea if anything she was doing would help, but right now, it made me feel better. That was the most important thing. I walked with her to her car. She said nothing more to me, not even a goodbye, before starting her car and pulling away so fast that she kicked up gravel beneath the tires. As soon as she turned onto the road, the phone in my pocket rang.

CHAPTER 16

"Hi, Khadijah. I'm just checking in on you. How's it going?" It was Alton.

"Your grandmother just left the house." I watched as Glory's car disappeared up the road. "Thank you so much for introducing us."

"No problem," he said. "I'll be in town today and was wondering if you want to grab lunch."

The house cast a shadow over me. I looked up at it. I needed to be someplace else, and I knew Davida wouldn't mind. "That'll be nice. I'd love to have lunch with you."

When I told Davida I was leaving, she hugged me and told me to get cleaned up and get some rest. I pulled into the parking lot of the Valley Inn and sat in my car for a moment, breathing deeply. I pulled the mojo bag from my cleavage and held it in the palm of my hand. It didn't weigh much. It seemed to weigh almost nothing at all. Again, I held it to my nose and took a deep breath of its pungent, earthy smell. It calmed me. I stuck it back in my bra and got out of the car. When

I looked up, I noticed Mr. Xavier standing on the porch. He raised an eyebrow at me.

"How's your day going so far?" Something about the way he looked at me made me feel uneasy.

"It's been pretty uneventful. I just came back to get cleaned up."

He continued to stand there, staring at me. Part of me wanted to get in the car and drive away, but I needed to shower and change. "That mojo bag won't protect you from anything; you know that, right?"

I tried to swallow down the lump in my throat. "I don't see how what I have or don't have on me is any of your business." I knew I didn't even need to say that much to him. Yet I couldn't seem to stop myself from talking. I walked past him into the house without saying anything else. I felt him watching me as I closed the door behind me. A group of five people stood in the living room, looking at the travel brochures the Xaviers kept there. There was no sign of Mrs. Xavier, so I hurried through the living room and up the hallway to my room. I didn't feel safe until I was inside with the door closed. My heart raced, and my breathing was quick and panicked. I used to be so rational and together, but ever since we started working on this house, I felt like I was falling apart. I'd become a hysterical, irrational mess of a person. I took a few deep breaths, trying desperately to calm down. Once I calmed myself, I glanced around the room and noticed the curtains were open. I swore they were shut tight when I left the house that morning. I walked over to close them and noticed the window was unlatched. My heart began to hammer in my chest again.

The box of newspapers I had taken from the house was gone. I'd left it on the small table in the corner of the room. I looked under the bed and in the closet to make sure I hadn't stashed it anywhere before I left and forgotten. It was nowhere. I knew it wasn't in the car. I had left it in the room. Why would someone take it?

I was immediately suspicious of Mr. Xavier but knew better than to go out and accuse him of anything. That wouldn't get me anywhere. He would only deny it, and I had no evidence to prove otherwise. After being sure that the box was nowhere in the room, I sat on the bed, thinking. I didn't know where the time went, but I was pulled from my scheming by my cell phone ringing. It was Alton. I was late for lunch.

"Alton, I'm sorry. I'm leaving right now." My keys were still in my hand. I still looked a mess, but I needed to talk to someone who would believe me, and Alton seemed like that someone.

"I thought you were standing me up." His tone was light.

"No. I've just been so out of it that I lost track of time." I walked through the Valley Inn and out onto the porch. "I'll be there in five minutes."

"Is there anything you want me to order for you while I wait?"

I almost asked him to order me a whiskey but thought better of it. As I pulled out of the parking lot, I looked in the rearview mirror and swore I saw the silhouette of a man standing next to the house, watching me as I pulled away. He was not tall enough to be Mr. Xavier, and because of the angle of the sun, I could only see his silhouette. I tried not to think about it too hard. I was making a big deal of everything these days. He was probably just another guest. That's what I wanted to believe.

Alton stood when he saw me walking toward the table. As soon as I saw that he was wearing a dress shirt and slacks, I grew flush with embarrassment. I was still filthy from filling in that hole. I hadn't even checked myself in the mirror before going into the restaurant.

He smiled brightly when he saw me as if not noticing the state of my appearance. "It's so good to see you." He came around the table to greet me with a handshake.

"I'm sorry I look a mess." I slouched when I spoke, wanting to disappear into the floor. I wondered what the other guests in the restaurant might be thinking of me. The place wasn't fancy. It was a tiny bistro. The kind of place that served mostly sandwiches and salads. The patrons were a diverse crowd of people, but I was sure that I was the most inappropriately dressed.

Alton pulled out my chair. Once he had settled into the chair across from me, he took a sip of his iced tea. He set the glass down on the table methodically. "I don't mean to be rude, but you don't look like you're doing very well."

My neck and face grew hot. I exhaled. "That's what I wanted to talk to you about."

"My grandmother isn't helping you?" He kept his fingers around his glass, the condensation dripping onto his hand.

"No... I mean, yes. Her workings are helping, I think. There's so much going on and..." I looked down at the place setting in front of me.

The waitress wandered over with a broad smile on her face. "Are you ready to order?"

Alton held up his hand. "We need a few more minutes." He flashed a smile at her.

She nodded knowingly and moved on to the next table.

I wasn't even hungry. I was too anxious for food. "Do you think someone is trying to scare me off because they wanted the house?"

Alton didn't even think before shaking his head. "I doubt it. That thing sat on the market for ages. Nobody wanted to touch it. You know that."

I looked down at the menu, pretending I was interested in picking out something to eat. I didn't want to look him directly in the eye. "Are you sure no one else was trying to buy it? I'm not accusing you of anything. I'm looking into all possibilities, that's all." I looked up to see him looking at me with his mouth pressed into a firm line.

"No one wanted to buy that house for a reason. Now that you've bought it, you have to deal with the consequences of owning it." He pulled his eyebrows together, creasing his forehead. "There are consequences to every action we make. You know that, Khadijah."

His tone suddenly seemed condescending, and I didn't like that one bit. "Of course, I know that, but normally when you buy a house, you don't get threatened and terrorized afterward."

"Is what you're experiencing really a threat?"

"It certainly feels like one." I closed the menu. "You're the one who suggested that your grandmother help me out. I thought that meant that you thought I was being threatened too."

He shrugged. The movement was so slight it was almost imperceptible.

"Why the sudden change? Do you know something now that you didn't before?" I cocked my head at him and waited for an answer, studying his face.

"I haven't had a change of heart. I just want to make sure you're okay and not working yourself up. You might..." He paused. Then he lowered his voice, leaned forward, and said, "hurt yourself." He lowered his chin as if that meant something. "You're looking a bit rough."

"I'm renovating a house." My voice was a little too loud. The people at the table next to us turned and looked.

"I realize that." He looked around. "That's not what I'm talking about. I was wondering if something else has happened. My grandmother says you're dealing with something big." He spit out his words rapidly.

I crossed my arms. I wasn't sure who I could trust. "Someone broke into my room at the Valley Inn."

"Did you tell Doug and Gladys?"

I shook my head. "I was just so tired and shocked. I sat on my bed and zoned out for a while. That's why I was late." I looked down at my clothes. "And I look like this."

"What did they take?"

"Well, that's the weird thing. Remember how I told you I found all those newspapers in the house with pictures of Raoul in them?"

He nodded.

"Well, I had one of those boxes in my room, and that's all they stole."

"That's strange."

"My room is on the first floor, and I swear I saw someone outside the window. Anyway, that's how they got into my room. The window was unlocked." This time I leaned forward, gripping the edge of the table with my hands. "Just now, when I left, I swear I saw the same guy I saw at my window in the parking lot."

"Back at the Valley Inn?" He raised an eyebrow.

I nodded emphatically. "I don't know for sure. I'm having a hard time trusting myself right now, but I swear. He was just standing next to the building, watching me pull away."

"Because he wanted to break into your room again?"

"How should I know?" It came out with a little more force than I anticipated. Before I could say anything, the waitress came back over. I ordered the soup and salad without giving it much thought. I waited until she was out of earshot to continue. "I'm sorry." I rested my elbows on the table. "I'm just so stressed right now."

"Maybe you should go back to the city and get some rest."

"You sound like Davida. Your grandmother told me that even if I go someplace else, at this point, it won't matter. Whatever this is, it's going to follow me around. So, I'd rather keep it here than bring it with me back to my home."

"I understand." He thought for a moment. "I'll check in with my grandmother and see what's going on. I'll make sure she knows how dire the situation is for you."

"I think she already knows, but I appreciate that." I liked knowing Alton was watching out for me.

"Has anything else happened at the house?"

I shook my head. I didn't even know. I was in the house so briefly that I didn't have time to look around. And I don't even know if Davida would tell me if something was wrong at this point. She recognized how fragile I'd been. She probably just wanted to ensure I got out of this renovation project with my mental health intact. "Honestly, I had all these grand ideas for the house, but with all that is happening, I'm thinking that I might just fix it up and sell it like I do every other house."

He blinked at me blankly. "That might be harder than you think."

"What do you mean?"

"That house has a history. That's why no one bought it. No matter how much it's been renovated, I don't think you'll find a buyer."

"Come on. You're a real estate agent. Not everyone interested in buying a house is from the area. Only locals know the place's past." I tried to sound more confident than I was. If anyone who bought the house would experience the same things I had, I would feel guilty unloading it on them. But I also wanted to keep some of my sanity. "I did find something strange since the last time I talked to you. I wanted to show you the picture, but that newspaper is gone now." I shrugged.

"Anyway, there's a picture of Raoul and a woman in one of the papers. She looked familiar to me. I think the paper is from 1938."

He looked at me as if waiting for me to say something else. I realize I didn't have anything else to say. I only wanted to tell someone about the picture because it had been haunting my thoughts ever since I saw it.

I cleared my throat. Suddenly, I felt uncomfortable. "I suspect that whoever stole that box took it specifically because of that picture."

"If you know what the newspaper was, you can probably find the archives online."

Why hadn't I thought of that? "You're right. If it's a real newspaper, there should be some record of it somewhere."

"There should be records of all of the newspapers."

Suddenly, I had something to do. I didn't know how productive it would be, but it felt concrete if I could figure out if the papers were even real. "You're a genius." I went to stand up. My chair scraped loudly on the floor.

Alton didn't move. "I thought you were going to stay for lunch."

"I'm sorry. You're right." I sank back into my seat. "I'm starving." On a normal day, I would've enjoyed the lunch and the conversation a lot more than I did on that day because on that day, I couldn't get Raoul, the house, and that mysterious picture out of my mind.

CHaPTer 17

After lunch, I ended up back at Warner Manor. The workers had made so much progress in such a short time. Just about everything was torn apart. The house was stripped down to the bones in some rooms. I walked through all of what they accomplished in such a short time. "There you are." I walked up to Davida and JJ, who were enthralled in conversation.

They both looked at me with wide, surprised eyes.

"I thought you went home to rest." JJ looked at Davida with a concerned expression. She motioned for him to leave us alone. He walked off quickly. Before he was out of sight, he turned around and said, "You need to take care of yourself, Khadijah. You haven't been the same since we started this project."

I wasn't sure what he meant. "I am taking care of myself."

"He's right, you know." Davida grabbed my arm and guided me through the workers to a small room that was empty now. "I thought I told you to get some rest."

"I can't rest in that place."

"Then find another place or go home. It's not rocket science, Khadijah. You're making a disaster of yourself staying here. Everyone can see it."

"Okay, I'll leave," I said without knowing where I was going to go. "I have to get something first." I hurried up the narrow hallway off the living room and flung the door open. I wanted to get another box of newspapers to look through in that room. At least, last time I looked, there were but this time, I flung the door open to find an empty room.

I ran out of the room up the hallway. "Davida, what happened to all the newspapers?"

She looked at me with confusion on her face. "What newspapers?"

I couldn't believe she was asking me that question. "The newspapers that were in that room." I pointed. "The boxes of newspapers we thought were Raoul's art project."

"They should be in there." She obviously didn't think this was as much of an emergency as I did. "Maybe one of the guys threw them out. I doubt it though. We haven't done anything in that room." She strolled into the empty room and looked around. "On the plus side, that's less junk for us to deal with."

I couldn't believe she was referring to it as junk. "If you're right, and they were part of a project he'd been working on, they could've been worth a lot."

"What about the ones in the attic?" she asked me.

I'd almost forgotten about those. Without answering her, I spun around and ran up the hallway. I raced up the stairs and made my way to the attic. I had no idea whether Davida was following me or not. When I got to the top of the stairs, I could already see that the room was empty, just like the room downstairs. Every single box was gone. The wood plank floors were covered in dust, like there were never any boxes there.

I turned around to find Davida standing behind me. Our eyes met. "I don't understand. Where did they all go if no one threw them away?"

She shook her head. "I'll ask the guys, but I don't see how they would've thrown them out without me noticing."

The dumpster outside had been there for a couple of days. I went running down the stairs. I had to check it. I passed JJ in the hallway.

"What's wrong?" He stepped to the side to let me by.

I didn't stop to answer. I couldn't answer. I needed to see if it was true. I ran downstairs and straight out the front door. The dumpster was too tall for me to see into, but I could stand on the ledge on the side of it and just peek over the edge. It was nearly full, and I knew the truck was going to come to take it away today. If the newspapers were inside, I needed to rescue them before that happened. I couldn't see any cardboard boxes amongst all the construction debris, but they could've been buried inside. If only I could get into the dumpster to see. They had to be there. They couldn't have disappeared. I hadn't imagined them.

"Are they there?" Davida stood behind me with her hands on her hips.

"I don't understand. This doesn't make any sense. You can't tell me this makes sense to you." I shook my head and ran a hand over my hair. "You saw the newspapers too, didn't you?"

Davida stepped up onto the ledge of the dumpster and looked in too. "Of course, I saw the newspapers. You're not losing your mind. They really did exist. But I have no idea where they are."

Tears pricked my eyes. I was surprised to feel the sting as one rolled down my cheek. All this time, I was trying so hard to be the successful one. The good one. The one who had made it against all odds. Now, this house owned by my favorite artist was destroying my mental health. I was the crazy one. I was the one who was falling apart despite everything. And that was terrifying. Suddenly, my knees felt weak. I squatted on the driveway with my head in my hands. Instead of trying to hold me up, Davida squatted with me. She was speaking, but I had no idea what she was saying.

"Khadijah!"

I looked up to see Davida staring into my face. Her eyes flicked back and forth. "I'm going to take you back to the city."

I nodded slowly. Nothing felt better than the idea of going back to the city in that moment. I wanted to go back in time to the moment that flyer about the auction arrived in my mailbox. If I had ignored it, none of this would have happened to me. I would still have control of my life. I wouldn't have sunk an enormous sum of money into a doomed project.

I moved like a zombie to Davida's truck. She helped me climb in. As I moved, I could feel the mojo bag shifting in my bra, and I laughed. So far, it hadn't done me any good at all. "You just sit here and relax. I'll be right back."

I watched Davida walk back up to the house. She disappeared inside. I stared at the manor. When I'd first seen it, I'd seen so much potential. It looked like exactly what I needed in my life. Looking up at it now, I only saw it as the thing that finally broke me. I wanted to get as far away from it as possible, but part of me still felt drawn to it. The conflict tore at me. When I thought of finally leaving it, I felt dizzy with fear, but nausea roiled up in me when I thought of staying here. I closed my eyes and breathed deeply. I managed to pull myself together by the time Davida returned to the truck.

She wore a falsely reassuring smile. "Do you want to go by the bed and breakfast to get your things?"

"Yeah." Only moments ago, I would've told her just to take me straight back home because I couldn't deal with this for even a second longer. Now I was feeling a bit more clearheaded. I wasn't even sure if I wanted to go at all.

Davida looked at me skeptically. "Are you sure?"

I nodded definitively. I rested my head against the window and watched the scenery whizzing by. Everyone drove too quickly on these small country roads, including Davida. She rambled on about how she thought the crew would be okay and how she had put JJ in charge. Normally, these were all things I would've been concerned about, but these days, how the project was going was the last thing on my mind.

"This place is cute." Davida pulled into the parking space right in front of the door. "I wouldn't mind staying here myself."

"You wouldn't say that if you had experienced what I have here."

She raised an eyebrow at me. "This place too?"

"You have no idea."

I expected to see Mr. Xavier on the porch. It seems like he had a knack for showing up out there every time I pulled up, but he wasn't there today.

Davida followed me inside. She paused in the living room to look around. "It's so cozy in here."

I knew what she meant. I thought the same thing when I arrived. Then I hadn't been threatened and terrified yet. I walked with a determined stride through the living room and up the hallway to my room. I was grateful that Mr. Xavier was nowhere to be seen. I heard some noises coming from the kitchen but ignored them. Davida walked next to me.

"It seems cozy until you actually stay here and realize how creepy it is," I said under my breath.

When we got to my room, I could feel something was amiss before I opened the door. I turned the doorknob, which wasn't locked. "Someone's been in here."

"How do you know?" Her eyes searched my face.

"I would never leave it unlocked."

At first glance, the room seemed to be just as I left it. I crossed the room to open the curtains and made sure the window was still locked. I stood, looking out of the window at the trees only a few feet away, their spindly branches reaching upward. I searched among their trunks for the dark figure I swore had been watching me. The sun came out from behind the clouds, and as it shone at an angle through the windowpane, I saw the streaks on the glass. Someone had traced the number eight on my window. I looked at the looping shape, my heart pounding. Suddenly, there was a hand on my shoulder, and I jumped.

"Calm down." I had forgotten Davida was even in the room with me. She peered out the window. "What are we looking at?"

My heart was still pounding in my chest as I pointed at the glass. "Someone wrote the number eight on the glass. Can you see it?"

She squinted and leaned in. "Oh yeah. I see it now. That's weird."

"I don't understand what it means, but it keeps showing up."

"Like the graffiti at the house," Davida added.

I turned around and scanned the room again. I had been so concerned with the idea that someone had gotten in through my window that I totally missed something when I walked in the first time. Sitting on the rocking chair in the corner of the room was an old newspaper. The pages yellowed with age.

"What's that?" I asked, walking toward it. I looked down at it, too fearful to touch it at first. The *Memphis Gazette* was written across the top of the page. June 26, 1934. I looked at Davida, who was standing next to me, looking as confused as I felt.

"I thought you said all the newspapers were gone."

"I thought they were." I reached out and picked up the paper. I unfolded it carefully and began flipping through it, scanning the pages.

"What are you looking for?"

"You know what I'm looking for: Raoul. Just like in all the other papers."

It didn't take long to find him. This time, he was standing alone at the edge of the forest. His dark eyes stared out at me. I saw something in his eyes, a recognition that I hadn't noticed before. It was like he could see me. He was looking through time at me.

"There he is again." Davida's voice was an anchor holding me in the here and now.

"Do you feel like he can see you?"

I felt her eyes on me. "Khadijah, it's only a picture."

I knew it was only a picture, but somehow it felt like so much more than that. I nodded. "I know, but every time I find one of his pictures, I feel like he can see me."

Looking at his stern face sent shivers down my spine. I was about to close the newspaper when something inside me told me to turn the page. When I did, I couldn't believe what I saw.

CHAPTER 18

D avida took in a sharp breath. "Wait a minute." She leaned over to get a closer look. "That looks like you."

The woman staring up at me from an almost one-hundred-year-old newspaper did indeed look very much like me. I knew that heart-shaped face and prominent chin because I saw it every morning in the mirror. Her hair was cut into a short straight bob that was popular in the day. She stood on a city street in a dark-colored dress that went just past her knees, holding her black purse in front of her body. Looking at the photo felt intensely personal. I fought the irrational urge to hide it from Davida.

"How is this possible?" She'd asked what I was thinking. "I don't understand what's happening."

I couldn't speak. I couldn't move. I could only stand there staring into the dark eyes that looked like my own.

She leaned over, her arm brushing mine, to get a closer look. "Could this be a distant relative?"

"I don't know. She looks so much like me." I held the photo closer to my face. The more I stared at her, the more she seemed to come alive until I swore I saw her eyes move. I dropped the newspaper and jumped back, bumping into Davida as I did.

"What happened?"

"Nothing. I can't take this anymore." I held my shaking hand to my mouth and swallowed a sob.

Davida picked up the newspaper, still mesmerized by the photo. "She looks frighteningly like you. She even has the same mole under her eye." Davida turned the page to face me. I only looked at it briefly before averting my gaze.

The paper crinkled as she looked through the other pages.

"This is wild. We have Raoul Bonnaire on this page, and then on the next page—I swear this is you, but how is that possible?" She looked around the room. "How did this even get here? I thought you said all the newspapers were gone."

"They were gone. They were all gone. This wasn't here when I left the room."

"Do you think someone broke in and put it here?" There was a knock on my door, and both of us jumped.

"Who's that?" Davida whispered.

"I don't know." There was no reason for anyone to be knocking on my door.

Davida put the newspaper on the end table and walked to the door. "Who is it?" she called out.

"It's just me, Gladys." I was relieved to hear Mrs. Xavier's voice. Davida looked back at me, and I nodded for her to open the door.

Mrs. Xavier stood in the doorway with a box in her hand. She wore a confused expression on her round face. "Someone dropped this off for you earlier. He said it was important."

Davida looked at me. I shrugged. "Maybe Alton left something for me. He's the only one I can think of that knows I'm here."

Davida looked back at Mrs. Xavier. "Did he give you a name?"

"I think you're right. I think he said his name was Alton or maybe Allen. I'm terrible with names." Her voice raised when she was unsure of what she was saying.

"Okay. Thank you," I said.

Davida took the box from her.

"He was such a nice young man. Good-looking too." Mrs. Xavier smiled as if in on a secret neither of us knew. After a moment of uncomfortable silence, she continued. "Well, I'll leave you to it." She pulled the door closed.

Davida set the box on the bed. "What do you think is in it?"

"I don't know—newspapers." I lifted the flaps to open it. Inside lay what looked like a dark bundle of fabric.

"What is it?" Davida asked.

I shook my head. Looking at the piece of fabric filled my heart with a kind of familiar dread. "I don't understand." I plunged my hands into the box and pulled out the exact same dress I had dug up the day before.

Davida gaped. "Wait a minute. Alton sent you that? How is that possible?"

An image of me running through a field on a hot day fluttered through my mind. My heart beat like a jackhammer in my chest. My throat was dry and sore. I wanted to yell, but I couldn't. My vocal cords constricted, choking back any sound I tried to make. Fear gathered in my chest. Looking back, I couldn't see what I was running from, but I could feel it close behind me.

"You look like you're in a completely different world." Davida stared at me.

I looked around and saw that I wasn't running from anyone. I was standing in my room at the Valley Inn. Still, my heart pumped wildly, and my throat was parched. "I'm fine. It was just like—" I let out a deep sigh. "It was just like I was having a daydream, but it was a nightmare."

"So, a kind of waking nightmare?" Davida returned her gaze to the dress.

"It's the dress. The one I dug up that showed up in my room on its own." I reached into the box, my hands trembling. "I swear I left it in my car." The stiff, crinkled fabric falling open felt like a bad omen.

"Does this mean Alton was behind all of this all along?" Davida's revelation knocked the wind out of me.

"There's a letter in here." Davida pulled a piece of paper from the bottom of the box.

I took the paper from her. It had degraded over time. The narrow cursive text had faded in places, making it difficult to read.

I read it out loud. "For my love, I am nothing without you. Though I am aware of the sorrow you claim I bring, I continue to try to the best of my ability to bring you the joy you long for. If you are so headstrong that you do not let me do that, it is impossible for us not to have conflict. I love you, and because of that, no matter how much time passes, you will always be mine. This eternal truth cannot be changed. We are beings drawn to each other. You will never escape my orbit. Our pull toward each other is too great. Run if you insist, but all pathways will always lead back to me. With undying love, Raoul."

"That's intense." Davida read the piece of paper over my shoulder. "I guess it's something else for the museum. If you still want to have a museum dedicated to..." She nodded toward the page.

The words in the letter pained me. My soul vibrated with anger that I shouldn't have felt. I could only stare down at the cramped text on the page in silence, my mind slowly processing the meaning of the words.

"How did Alton get the dress, and why did he drop it off here? It doesn't make sense." That's when I realized I didn't have to wonder. I dug my phone out of my pocket. I sent a quick text to him, thanking him.

Me: Thanks for the package you left at the Valley Inn for me.

Alton: ?

Me: Mrs. Xavier said you left a box for me.

Davida looked over my shoulder as I texted him. "He's lying."

"I believe him. Why would he lie about this?" My phone rang. I answered.

"I didn't send you anything." He sounded so serious. "Don't open it."

"It's too late for that."

"That wasn't smart. I wouldn't open any unexpected packages if I were you." He paused, and I could hear people cheering in the background. "What was in it?"

My laughter was forced. "Don't worry. It was just a dress and a letter Raoul wrote to Martina."

"Who would send you something like that?"

"That's what I'm trying to figure out. Mrs. Xavier said he was a nice young man who gave her your name."

"My name? Why would they give my name?" he asked.

"Probably to make sure I opened it." The implications were just starting to dawn on me. Someone really was watching me. They knew I trusted Alton, so they gave his name when they left the box. "I'm scared."

I heard some talking in the background. "I want you to go see my grandmother. I'll text you the address, and then I'll let her know

you're coming. We need to get all of this done as quickly as possible."
Something scraped against the receiver, the sound reverberating in my
ear. "I don't have time to talk now."

I looked at Davida. "I'm supposed to be heading back to the city."

"You can't do that. You can't go anywhere until my grandmother
has finished her work with you." His words were more urgent. "I'm
serious. It's really important. If you leave now, things will only get
worse for you."

I looked at Davida, who was watching me with one eyebrow raised.
"He says I can't go anywhere," I whispered to her.

"You can't. You have to stay right here," he reiterated. "I have to go.
I'll send you her address, and once I'm through here, I'll call you. We'll
get together." The line went silent for a moment, and I thought he had
hung up, but then he started speaking again. "Khadijah, this is serious.
You can't go anywhere. Promise me you'll stay here."

"Okay. Message received. I'll stay here." I looked at Davida, who was
shaking her head.

"What do you mean you'll stay here?" she asked as I hung up the
phone.

"Alton says I have to stay for his grandmother to finish her working
for me. He says if I go, it'll ruin everything." I looked down at the piece
of paper in my hand again. "So, it looks like I'm staying."

Davida shook her head again. "I can't believe this. You need to go
back to the city today."

"I can't now. I asked Glory to do a job for me, and I need to stay
here till it's done. Once it is, I'll go home. You and the crew can finish
up this job yourselves, and I'll go back home and get out of everyone's
hair."

She looked at me with doubtful eyes. "You promise?"

"I just said I promised. Since when do I go back on my word?"

"Do you want a list?" She laughed.

CHAPTER 19

D avida was reluctant, but I convinced her to take me to Glory's
house. I'm not sure what I expected, maybe a little shack out in
the woods with skulls on the fence posts. I didn't expect a bright yellow
two-story house just outside of town with wooden steps leading up to
a tidy porch. A horseshoe and bundle of elder flowers hung over the
door. Her beat-up car sat in the driveway.

"You're doing this on your own. Just make it quick," Davida said
as I got out of the truck.

The floorboards of the porch creaked when I stepped up onto it.
Glory opened the door before I had a chance to knock. She didn't
smile when she saw me. Instead, she looked over my shoulder at Davida's truck. "Is your friend coming inside?"

I shook my head. "She wants to wait out here."

Glory gave a nod before showing me into her home. It smelled of
sandalwood and pipe tobacco. The living room was bright and open,
with lace sheers on the windows and the kind of antique furniture you

feel like you shouldn't sit on. I hesitated when she motioned toward the cream-colored French provincial sofa for me to sit down.

"Go on then. Give me that box and take a seat." She smiled, and I saw a twinkle in her eyes.

I handed it to her and sat on the stiff sofa.

"I dug this dress up the other day, and then someone left it at the Valley Inn for me."

She raised her eyebrow. Then she sat in the hot-pink wingback chair across from me and opened the lid. She pulled out the dress, and the fabric rustled as it unfolded, revealing its length. The letter inside the box fluttered to the floor. Noticing it, she reached down and picked it up. I watched her as she read the letter. When she had finished, she looked up at me.

"There's something else in the box." I'd brought the newspaper with me because I thought it was important that she see it.

She checked the bottom of the box and pulled out the newspaper.

I got up and took it from her. "There is a picture that looks like me." Carefully, I turned the pages to show her the image. "And look at the date."

She looked at the photo for a good long time, taking the newspaper from me and squinting at the page. Occasionally, she would glance at me.

I felt uncomfortable standing there, wondering what would happen next.

Then she folded the newspaper carefully and stuck it back into the box. She did the same with the dress and the letter. She looked at me, her dark brown eyes soft with motherly emotion. "Child, this is bigger than I originally thought." She reached out and took hold of my hand. "I have to work quickly. There's no time." Glory got up and walked with determination across the room to the doorway. Realizing I was looking at her, she turned. "Do you still have your mojo bag?"

I reached into my shirt and pulled it from my cleavage.

"Good. I want to give you something a bit more powerful to work with it. Wait here." She disappeared through the door. I could hear her walking around in the other room. Cupboard doors opened and closed. Paper rustled. Unsure of what to do, I stood in the middle of the living room, almost afraid to move. I could see Davida sitting in the truck out of the window. When I did decide I could finally walk around, the floorboards creaked loudly under my feet. After what felt like forever, Glory came back, holding a brown paper sack.

"I'm going to meet you at the house at sunset. Before I do, I want you to steep these and drink the tea." She opened the bag to reveal a bunch of herbs.

I stuck my nose into the bag, and a pungent smell met my nostrils. I drew back. "What's in it?"

She grimaced at me. "Something that will protect you."

"I won't drink something if I don't know what it is. For all I know, you might be trying to kill me." My eyes met hers.

Glory drew her head back and scowled at me. "You think that's what I'm trying to do? I'm here helping you when no one else is, and you're accusing me of trying to kill you." She crumpled the opening of the bag closed and began to walk away.

I knew she was right; no one else had attempted to help me. I couldn't let her go. "I'm sorry. I'm sorry. I'm under a lot of pressure and don't know what to do."

She turned around, her face still hard. I knew I needed to do some more convincing.

"Of course, I'm grateful for everything you've done for me." A tear rolled down my cheek. I wiped it away, feeling embarrassed that I was crying over this. "Of course, I'll drink the tea. I'll do whatever you tell me to do as long as you promise you can make this stop."

Her stern expression melted. She held her hand out and gave me the paper bag of herbs. "Boil some water and steep these for ten minutes. Have it ready for drinking when I meet you at—" She paused for a moment and looked out the window. "At six o'clock."

I nodded. "Should I wait until you come before I drink it?"

"Yes." She thrust her hand into the side pocket of her tunic and pulled out a shiny black claw. A single black feather was tied to the ankle. "Take this for protection." She extended it toward me.

I didn't want to take it. Just looking at the black, scaly skin and curled talons sent a shudder through me.

She thrust her arm out toward me again, insisting. "This will protect you. Take it."

I reached into my cleavage and pulled out the small red mojo bag she had given me earlier. "I already have this."

She narrowed her eyes at me. "I know you have that, and now I'm giving you this too. A person in your situation should never turn down additional protection. You need as much as you can get."

The idea of walking around with an animal's foot did not make me feel protected. It made me feel disgusted, but I took it from her anyway.

"This crow's foot will keep you safe. Carry it with you all the time." She raised her chin toward me as she spoke. "Go now. I have to prepare for tonight."

I felt like I was in a daze as I wandered down from the front porch back out to the truck, where Davida waited for me. Davida looked at the crowfoot in my hand and wrinkled her face with disgust. "What is that?"

"It's supposed to protect me." I extended it toward her.

She shook her head. "Put that thing away." She put the truck into drive and pulled away from the curb.

"She gave me a tea to drink. She said I have to drink it to get ready for the ceremony we're performing tonight."

"Ceremony? You've gone and lost your mind. You used to have sense." She turned and looked at me for a few seconds. "Don't drink anything that woman gives you and no ceremonies."

"All right. All right." I held up my hands as if I was telling her to stop.

"Don't 'all right, all right' me and then ignore my advice. I'm worried about you."

"I know, and I'll go back home as soon as all of this is over. I have to take care of it here first though." Surprisingly, she didn't try to talk any more sense into me as she drove me back to the Valley Inn. Even though she was silent, I could still feel the worry radiating off her.

When I climbed out of the truck in the parking lot, she only said, "Be smart," as I closed the door. I watched her pull away before turning to go inside.

As I stepped into the Valley Inn's cozy living room, a deep voice said, "Are you doing okay?"

I jumped, my hand still on the doorknob. Mr. Xavier stood in the living room with his hands in his pockets next to the sofa. I had the feeling that he might've been standing there waiting for me. "Yeah, I'm fine."

The confusion must've come through in my voice because he decided to give an explanation for his question. "My wife told me someone dropped some stuff off here for you."

I didn't see how it was any of his business, but I still answered. "That's right. Why?"

He shrugged. Then he looked around the living room as if making sure no one else was listening before he walked toward me. The sound of his footfall seemed to amplify as soon as he stepped from the carpet to the wood near the entryway. "This isn't a game."

I had no idea what he was talking about. "I know. Who says I'm playing a game?"

"Things are happening in town, and that's partially because you stirred them up. Do you know what you're getting yourself into?" He looked at the bag of herbs in my hand. "What's that?"

"None of your business." I hardened my voice with indignation. "I'm not playing any games here. I wish whoever was trying to scare me away would just leave me alone."

He stepped toward me again, closing the distance between us. "They would if you would just go home."

"It's too late for that now."

"It is never too late." He stepped closer to me again.

I took a step back.

"You don't understand what you're getting into." I could smell his sour breath as he spoke.

He was right. I had no idea what I was getting into, and that was terrifying. "Why don't you tell me?"

He snorted, throwing his head back slightly. "The less you know, the better for you. There's evil in that house. There always has been. It would be best for you to walk away from it and never look back."

"Do you know what happened to Raoul? Do you know about the newspapers?"

"I don't know anything about any newspapers or what happened to Raoul. What I do know is that no one wanted that house for a reason."

That house called to me like I was supposed to have it, but now I regret setting foot inside. It was like a disease eating away at my soul, taking me over. A deep well of sadness opened inside of me because in that moment, I began to realize that no matter what I did, I could never go home. I belonged to the house now. I didn't have the energy to talk to him, so I turned and walked away.

"You best go home. You'll regret it if you don't," he said as I walked out of the living room.

It was only when I was finally alone in my room that I could let the emotions flood out. My legs felt like they could no longer hold me. I slid down the door to the floor, pulled my knees into my chest, and hugged myself. If I could've gone back in time, I would've changed everything. I would've never bought this house in the first place.

I cried for a while because sometimes you just need to let it all out. When I was done, I got up and immediately went to the bathroom to wash my face. I stood in the bathroom, looking at myself in the mirror, my face bleary, my eyes rimmed in red from crying, and took a few deep breaths. When I left the bathroom, I caught a glimpse of someone looking through the window just opposite the bathroom door at me. The window was small, and the sun shone through it, so brightly that I could only make out a silhouette. As soon as they realized I was looking back at them, they turned and ran away.

I went out of my room and ran up the hallway, through the living room, and out the front door. I sprinted around the building through the grass, the cool air burning my lungs. When I got to the window, there was no one there. I scanned the area and saw nothing. I ran to the tree line. The trees were tall and dense, with a lot of underbrush. Peering into the shadows, I saw no one. "Leave me alone!" I called into the woods.

A crow cawed in the treetops.

I stood looking into the woods, hoping to see someone but too afraid to venture in among the trees. The longer I stood out there listening to nothing, the more I began to think that I hadn't seen anyone at all outside my window. I traced my steps back to the inn. I walked right up to the window I had just seen the person at and looked through it. Inside, I saw my room looking warm and inviting. I looked down at my feet, hoping to see footprints where he had once stood, but there was no evidence that anyone had ever been there. Then I caught sight of it in the dust at the bottom corner of the windowpane. Someone had used their finger to write a perfect figure eight.

CHAPTER 20

I stopped at a local coffee shop to get a large cup of hot water and dumped the herbs Glory had given me into it. They steeped as I drove up to Warner Manor, releasing their pungent odor into the car. The smell was oddly familiar, comforting even. When I got to Warner Manor, Davida was just getting into her truck.

"You know I don't like any of this." The creases between her eyebrows deepened when she spoke.

"You've already made that clear." I got out of my car with my cup of hot water in my hands. The crow's foot remained in my shirt pocket, and my red mojo bag was tucked safely into my bra. I should've been fully protected from any sinister forces that were after me, but I felt as vulnerable as a newborn baby.

Davida glanced down at the cup and shook her head. "I shouldn't leave you here."

"But you will because you have things to do, and you know I'm grown and can handle this on my own."

She pressed her lips together as if keeping herself from protesting again. She grabbed my arm so hard I nearly spilled the hot water in my hand. "Don't do anything stupid." It sounded more like a plea than anything else.

"Don't worry, I won't."

I didn't see her get into her truck and drive away. I was walking up to the house when I heard the gravel crunching beneath her truck tires. I stepped inside. It was empty and quiet. The setting sun cast a faint orange glow through the windows. As I stood with the cup in my hand, I remembered the box Mrs. Xavier had given me, sitting in the back seat of my car. When I left, I felt like I should take it with me, but I didn't know why. Now, I felt the desire to get it. I left my cup of hot water on the step and went outside into the soft light of dusk to retrieve the box. As I crossed the gravel driveway with the box in hand, I felt like I wasn't alone. I felt eyes roving over my back, taking in every part of me. But when I turned and looked, I saw nothing, only a few trees in the front yard, the recently mowed grass, and the street beyond. I was alone. With a new sense of uneasiness, I ran up the steps to the porch and ducked inside, shutting the door and locking it behind me. My heart hammered in my chest, and my breathing was rapid. I tried desperately to get it under control. What time was it? I wasn't even sure. I hoped Glory would show up soon.

When you're scared, your senses become elevated. Even the smallest sound sets you on edge. That's the way I felt as I stood with my back against the door.

I placed the box on the floor in front of me and opened it, revealing the drab, faded fabric of the dress. I held it up by its shoulders and examined it. The uneven stitches suggested that it had been sewn by hand. Someone had made this. Maybe that same someone was the one who wore it. I wondered who that was. I felt so curious about what it might be like to be that woman that I slipped out of my clothes and into the dress. I can't explain exactly how it happened. It was almost like I was in a trance brought on by the feel of the fabric in my hands. The dress embraced me as I slid it over my head, calming my racing heart. It didn't matter if anyone else was there with me because I knew that in this dress, I was safe. I stood in the foyer, running my hand down the skirt, smoothing the stiff fabric. The shoulder seams hit at exactly the right place. It was almost as if it had been custom-made for me. I wished for a mirror so I could see what I looked like. That's what I was doing when a knock on the door sent a shot of adrenaline through me. I jumped, my hand on my heart.

"Who's there?" I called.

"It's me. Let me in." Glory's tired voice came through the door.

I fumbled with the lock but finally opened the door. Relief washed over me when I saw Glory standing in front of me. She held a jar of red dirt.

"I'm glad you're here. I hate being in this place by myself." I stepped aside to let her in.

"Did you drink it?" She looked at both of my hands, expecting to see something. When she saw they were empty, her disappointed gaze landed on my face.

"It's here. I got some hot water from a coffee shop." I picked the disposable cup up from the steps. A potpourri of herbs floated in the cup.

She took it from me, surprising me when she took a sip. Bits of green herbs stuck to her upper lip, and she smacked her lips together. Then she handed it to me. "It's steeped for long enough. Drink it."

I looked down at the cup. "What is it?"

She stepped in, closing the gap between us. "If we're going to do the ceremony correctly and reverse this hex, we must perform every part of the ritual. These herbs have magical properties. Every plant does. They can protect you by drawing in the good and repelling the bad. They'll give you good health and good luck."

I looked down at the cup in my hands with suspicion.

"What's wrong? Don't you trust me?" The annoyance that tinged her words was unmistakable. "I don't have to help you."

"It's just that," I stammered.

She threw up her hands. "Fine. I'll go then." She turned around and reached for the doorknob.

My hand was on her shoulder before I could even stop myself. "Don't. I'll drink it."

She turned around, and I held the cup to my lips. I took a deep breath before chugging down all the liquid. Bits of the herbs got into my mouth, pricking my tongue and catching in my throat. I tried my best not to swallow many of them. Some of the bitter tea dribbled from my mouth. When I was done, I tipped the cup toward her so she could look inside to prove that I had drunk it all.

Glory nodded affirmatively. "Very good." She held up the jar of red dirt. "Now we can get started."

"What's that?" I asked. Bitterness lingered in my mouth.

"It's red brick dust. It'll keep the evil out." She reached for a sack sitting by the door I hadn't noticed before and pulled out some black candles encased in glass. She put them on the floor in the middle of the foyer. She pulled out a bottle of what looked like cologne and doused it on her hands as she mumbled what sounded like a Bible verse.

"What are you doing?" She stopped what she was doing, her stare like daggers through me.

"Are you going to keep asking me questions, or are you going to let me do this?"

"I just want to know what's happening." The herbs felt warm and fiery in my stomach. I put my hand on my belly and took a deep breath.

"I'll tell you when you need to do something. Right now, you should let me do the work." She held up her jar of red dirt. "I'm going to take care of every way into this place." Mumbling something under her breath that I couldn't quite hear, she poured a line of dust across the threshold at the front door. "See that. No one can cross that now. We must do this so our work won't be interrupted." She looked at me as if trying to read what I was thinking. "I'm going to take care of the rest of the house. You can have a seat for now and relax." She motioned to the staircase behind me.

I walked over to the dusty stairs and sat down.

She stood, watching me. "Good." She walked into the living room.

"I'll be here when you're done." I still had the empty cup in my hand. I set it down on the step next to me and listened to Glory's footsteps as she walked around the house. I couldn't imagine how a little bit of dirt could keep anyone out, but she seemed convinced it would work. It wouldn't hurt anything besides giving us something to sweep up in the morning. She seemed to be gone a little too long, and I wondered where she was. I couldn't hear her walking around anymore.

I tried to stand but felt dizzy, so I lowered myself back to my resting place. My thoughts were swimming. My eyelids drooped, and I kept drifting off. Was it because I had such a stressful few days? I angled my gaze down at the cup sitting next to me. The dark green herbs coated the inside wall. Had Glory drugged me?

No sooner had the thought entered my mind than a wave of nausea passed over me. I leaned forward, holding my stomach, certain I might vomit. I held my head in my hands. I was barely able to keep my eyes open. No matter how hard I tried, they grew heavier and heavier.

Eventually, I was only looking at the world through tiny slits, and then my eyelids closed completely, almost as if beyond my control, and I was plunged into another time.

CHAPTER 21

S ometimes, dreams can feel more real than reality. That's how I feel about the dreams I had at that moment. I stood in a field of amber grass beneath a bright blue sky dotted with cotton-candy clouds. A man stood with his back to me on the other side of the field. He wore a black suit on his slender frame. I felt drawn to him. I walked toward him, lifting my feet high in the tall grass. The coarse fabric of my dress swung around my legs. The closer I got to him, the closer I wanted to be. Eventually, I broke into a run. When I had finally reached him, I extended my hand, placing it on his shoulder. The fabric of his suit jacket was silky and smooth. Beneath it, I could feel the bones protruding from his shoulders. As soon as I touched him, dread passed through me, and I felt like I had made a terrible mistake. I wanted to rewind time and run back across the field away from him. Before I knew it, he was turning around. He didn't have a face at all. Where a face should have been, there was a hole as dark as the midnight sky with pinpricks of light like stars. Looking into that darkness reminded me of how small and insignificant I was. I opened my mouth to speak, but no words came out. Something jolted me, and I was pulled back into wakefulness.

CHAPTER 22

I thought I had only shut my eyes for a few minutes, so when I opened them, I was surprised to see Alton looking down at me. "What are you doing here?" I asked. My voice didn't feel like my own.

"My grandmother invited me." He cocked his head. "Are you okay?"

"Yeah, I'm great." Even as I spoke, I noticed myself shaking my head no, like a subconscious admission that I knew something wasn't quite right.

He raised an eyebrow.

I looked around. The walls seemed to wave back and forth. The ground beneath me rocked. "Where is she?" I leaned forward, holding my head. "I don't feel good."

"I'm sure you're going to be fine." He reached down as if wanting to take my hand. Confused, I reached up, and before I knew it, he was pulling me to my feet. Everything around me swayed. "Let's get you upstairs."

"Why?"

He put his arm around me, holding me up. I leaned my head against his chest. "My grandmother's up there. That's where we're going to do the ritual to make all of this stop."

I closed my eyes to blink but didn't want to open them again.

I leaned against Alton as we went up the stairs. I'm not sure why I went with him. I desperately wanted all this to end and saw the ritual as the only solution. "I feel funny."

"I know. It's going to be okay." He gripped me tighter as we walked up the last few stairs.

I stood at the top of the steps in the dark, looking down the hall where light bled into the darkness. We walked toward the light. I had no idea what this ritual was that Glory had in store, but I was anxious to get it done. The floorboards creaked under my feet as I went. I walked toward the soft glow at the end of the hallway. As we got closer, my heartbeat quickened, and a thin film of sweat formed on my forehead. My footsteps slowed.

"Is everything okay?" Alton asked.

I nodded even though my skin crawled with fear. "I just want to get this over with." I moved away from him, wanting to walk on my own now.

He looked at me with concern.

"I can manage."

"Okay." He let go of me but still held his arms out like he thought I might fall.

"I'm fine." My voice was firm this time, even though I knew I wasn't fine. I still felt woozy and off-kilter, but I needed to walk into the room on my own.

With Alton behind me, I approached the doorway, wondering what I might find inside. The room was aglow with a cluster of pillar candles sitting in its center. Wax spilled over their edges as their yellow flames danced, putting off plenty of light to fill the room and a lot of heat. Someone stood in the far corner of the room with his back to me. I turned to Alton, my mouth opened to ask a question, but he was talking before I could get my inquiry out.

"It's okay. He's here to see you."

I crinkled my forehead at him.

He nodded, urging me into the room, the hint of a smile playing across his face.

The form on the other side of the room stood still, looking at the floor.

I heard footsteps behind me and then a voice.

"Why did you bring her up without me?" Glory said.

I looked over my shoulder at her. She still had the jar in her hand, but it was empty now.

"I didn't want to wait any longer," Alton said. "We've already waited long enough."

"A few more minutes wouldn't hurt anything. Your generation is so impatient. You—"

"Kadijah." A deep voice interrupted Glory's complaints.

We all looked at the figure across the room. He turned slowly to face us, holding his thin arms out in a grand gesture. Raoul Bonnaire stood before me in the same dark suit and hat I'd seen him wearing the first time I found his photo in a newspaper. His slim face was timeless. His skin was smooth and without blemish. I gasped, putting my hand over my mouth and stepping back. When I did, I bumped into Alton, standing right behind me. "I don't understand..."

"Yes, you do," Raoul said, his voice like velvet. "You've always understood."

Memories of lives I'd lived before began to cycle through my mind. A woman walking through the forest, sneaking away from her family to meet her lover. The wet grass brushed the bare skin of her feet through her sandals. I hurry when I see him sitting on a rock by the river waiting for me. It's Raoul looking just as he does now.

A woman standing in a hot kitchen wearing many layers of clothes. I sweat as I stir the pot on the stove. The whole while, I'm cooking and thinking of Raoul and when I will see him again.

A woman rushing through a crowded street, crossing in front of horse-drawn carriages. I hold my skirts up so I don't trip. I'm hurrying to meet my boyfriend, overjoyed that we're finally reuniting.

I saw images like this again and again in my mind.

I turned to face Alton and Glory standing behind me. "I don't understand. You were in on this all along."

I looked around the room and saw eights painted on the walls again and again in red, dripping paint.

"You look beautiful in that dress. Do you remember the day I gave it to you?" Raoul asked.

I couldn't look at him. I didn't want to look at him ever again.

"Don't be afraid. My love for you is too great. Each time you leave me, I must wait so long before we can reunite. I do this," he gestured around the room, "to help you remember." He walked over to the wall and traced one of the painted eights. "You might think this is just a number, but it's so much more. Every curve represents us and how we are meant to be together for eternity. We are bound to one another. You will always find your way back to me."

I shook my head. Memories continued flooding into my mind. "Why did you help him?" I asked Alton.

"You're not the only person who wants to live forever. He promised me that much if I helped him get you back." Alton's smooth voice didn't seem so magnetic now.

My gaze shifted to Glory. Before I could ask her anything, she spoke. "What is this foolishness about living forever?"

A car door slammed outside, and everyone's heads turned in the direction of the sound.

Raoul looked out the window. "Someone is here," he said.

I heard another car door slam. Alton rushed through the room to join him at the window.

"Why don't they mind their own business?" Alton brought his fist down on the windowsill.

Within seconds, someone was at the door. The thud of knocking reverberated through the house.

"Who is it?" I asked, hoping someone was coming to rescue me.

"They can't get in." Glory held up her empty jar.

Maybe she was right, and they couldn't get in, but I hoped I could get out. Whatever Glory had given me was beginning to wear off, and I thought I might be able to escape. I spun on my heels and tried to run, but my feet got all tangled around each other. I fell to the floor in a clumsy heap. Alton ran over to me and grabbed my arm, yanking me to my feet.

There was another thump on the door. "We know you're in there!" a familiar voice called.

Still holding my upper arm, Alton returned to the window to look out. I saw three figures walking around the house. I could barely make them out in the moonlight. "Is that Mr. Xavier?" I asked.

No one answered me.

He pointed at us and spoke to the person beside him, a man I didn't recognize. Then he began to yell. "You can't hide from us." They both walked toward the house again.

"Don't worry," Glory said. "They'll never get in."

The thumping on the door grew louder.

Alton pulled me into the center of the room, where the heat from the candles was more intense. Raoul grabbed my hands, holding them. His flesh was cool and rough.

"I don't understand what's happening." I fell to my knees, my body too weak to support itself. It was as if the mere act of touching him was draining the life from me.

"Relax," he said. "Trust me, and it will all be okay."

"What if I don't?" I whispered.

He frowned. "You don't have a choice. You've never had a choice." As he spoke, more memories flooded back to me. The joy I'd seen in the lives before suddenly became intense fear. I was the woman who drowned herself in the river where she always met her lover. I was the woman who hung herself in the barn where she milked the cattle. I was the woman who threw herself off a building. I was the woman who fled this house and drove into a tree.

All of those women were me, and I'd chosen to cut each life short, but why? Pain rippled through me as he held my hands even tighter. I looked up at his face, pleading with him for mercy. "Don't." I wasn't even sure what I was asking him not to do.

Raoul's features slowly melted in on themselves. His skin oozed and dripped like candle wax down his neck, revealing layers of slick red tissue that undulated and twisted into a new form. His face scrambled and shifted, contorting into something otherworldly. Raoul was no human. He was something much different, a being like nothing I'd seen before. He looked like he'd crawled from the deepest, darkest parts of the ocean—some undiscovered life form adapted to survive where no other living creature could. I tried to draw away, but he held onto me tighter.

Glory shrieked with horror. She turned to run from the room.

Alton caught her, wrapping his arms around her torso. "It's okay, Grandma. Everything is going to be fine."

"No! Nothing here is fine. You lied to me." She swatted at him.

He leaned back, lifting her feet from the floor, and she tried desperately to kick him. He carried her to the back corner of the room and dropped her. She tried to run as soon as she hit the ground, but he pushed her backward into the wall. "I need you to stay here. I can't control what he'll do, so you have to promise me that you won't move."

She nodded.

"I mean it." He pulled a gun from the waistband of his pants and held it on her.

"Alton?" Betrayal washed over Glory's face.

"Don't make me use this." He backed away from her, keeping the barrel of the gun pointed in her direction. He went to the center of the room where the candles stood, their flames flickering.

There was another great thump, followed by Mr. Xavier yelling my name. "Khadijah! Khadijah!"

I tried to yank my hands away from Raoul, but he wouldn't let me go. I didn't dare look up at him. I swore it would break me mentally if I saw his face again.

"You can't escape. You can never escape me." He spoke somehow, but I wasn't sure where the words came from. Then, oozing tenacles burst from his head, reaching into the air.

I shuddered and tried desperately to wrench my arms from his grasp, but it was useless. I was certain I'd soon be dead.

Somewhere downstairs, glass shattered. Then there was another crash, closer this time, followed by the pounding of footsteps coming up the hall.

"I thought you said they couldn't get in." The panic in Alton's voice was evident.

"They shouldn't be able to," Glory said.

Mr. Xavier charged into the room with two other older men.

Alton raised his gun and shot once before he was tackled to the ground. The gun skittered across the floor.

One of the men doubled over, holding his abdomen, a red stain blooming on the fabric of his shirt.

Everything happened so quickly that it was hard to keep up with all the action around me.

There was another gunshot. I still have no idea where it came from, but Raoul let out a bloodcurdling cry and stumbled backward, letting go of my hands. I was surprised that a creature who had lived as long as he had could be taken down so easily. At that moment, my instincts took over. I ducked down to avoid the tentacles erupting from his head and ran at him, plowing my shoulder into his torso with all my might. The glass shattered as he hit the window behind him, and he toppled out, hitting the ground with a dull thud. I had built up so much momentum that I nearly fell out with him.

Alton flew to his feet. "What have you done?" He rushed to the window and looked out.

I looked out too, expecting to see Raoul splayed on the ground. He wasn't there. He had vanished.

"You just ruined my chance at eternal life." Anger blazed in his eyes as Alton wrapped his hands around my neck. A voice startled him before he could choke me.

"Stop," Glory yelled.

Alton froze and looked to his left to see Glory standing with a gun aimed at his head. "You wouldn't," he said.

"I don't know what you're trying to accomplish here, but, baby, this isn't the way." Glory's gaze flitted over to Mr. Xavier and his companion.

Both men stood against the wall.

The man who'd been shot lay on the floor, moaning with pain. Blood soaked through his white t-shirt.

"You can't lie to your grandmother and think you'll get away with it." The gun shook in her hands.

Alton laughed as he looked down the barrel of the gun. "You wouldn't shoot your only grandson."

His fingers still encircled my neck, and tears burned the back of my eyes. I didn't want to see anyone get shot. I had already seen too much.

No one moved.

"Don't you think this is all ending up this way for a reason?" Glory said.

Alton snarled. "You have no idea what you're saying." He let go of me, and I rushed to the other side of the room. I never thought I'd see the day I'd run into Mr. Xavier's arms, but that was exactly what I did.

Glory stepped closer to her grandson. "Stop this. I can't let you hurt this woman."

"Why not? You were going along with it before," he smirked.

"I was reversing a hex. I didn't know anything about ... that." She used the gun to motion to the broken window.

"You don't understand what he promised me. I could live forever. You could too. All we have to do is give her to him." He motioned to me, his eyes wild.

"What was that?" Disgust paced over Glory's face. "A demon?" Saying the word seemed to cause her physical pain.

Alton shook his head. "You're so old-fashioned. There are no demons."

Glory shook her head. "Yes, there are. I just saw one. You'll have to answer to God for this."

"When you live forever, you don't have to answer to anyone." He inched forward. "Give me the gun."

The gun trembled in Glory's hand. "Don't." A tear slid down her cheek. "You're my responsibility, and as God is my witness, I can't let you do this."

"She was always meant to be with him. I've just been helping destiny along." He took another step toward her. "You could live forever too."

"I don't want that." She stepped back, her boots scraping on the floorboards.

He cocked his head. "Come on. Everyone wants to live as long as they can." He lunged forward.

The gun went off. Alton looked down at his chest with a look of disbelief on his face. The red spot spread as he fell to his knees.

Glory dropped the gun and put her hand over her mouth. She let out a long, mournful wail. "What have I done? What have I done?" she yelled.

Alton fell forward onto the floor, and she rushed over to him, pulling at his body as if trying to sit him up. Tears flowed from her eyes. She looked over at me, pleading for help.

I felt nauseous. The room started to spin. I couldn't believe everything that had just happened. Everyone and everything else around me drifted away: Glory's sobbing, Mr. Xavier comforting her, the police sirens, the ambulance.

CHapTer 23

As I approached the doorway, I immediately regretted coming in the first place. Davida was right when she told me to stay away, but I needed answers. I'd decided not to press charges. I hadn't been sure what those charges would be and didn't want to make Glory's situation any worse than it already was. She'd thought she was helping me from the start and didn't know what Alton was really up to. Besides, I would've had an impossible time explaining who or what Raoul really was to the police. When the police did show up, we all told them that it was a scuffle that had gotten out of hand and no one was at fault. Of course, there was going to be an investigation, but I'd already decided not to tell them anything.

Alton lay with his head elevated. Someone was talking to him, but I couldn't see the person from where I stood. I rapped on the door before walking in, and Officer Moses came into view.

"Hello, Khadijah." He looked at me like he knew something I didn't.

"Hi." The word caught in my throat. I looked at Alton, wondering what he'd told his friend. "I can come back later. I mean, I don't want to interrupt you."

"You're not interrupting anything. I have to get going." He looked down at Alton. "When you're ready to tell me what really happened, I'm here." He angled a suspicious gaze at me before continuing. "Are you okay being alone with her?"

Alton nodded.

"All right then." Officer Moses walked toward me. "If you're responsible for this, I'll find out," he said as he passed me on his way to the door.

I didn't say anything. What was there to say? I doubted he'd believe me if I told him the truth. I listened to his footsteps as he walked down the hallway.

Alton grimaced at me.

We glared at each other in silence until we could no longer hear Officer Moses in the hall.

"You're lucky I didn't tell the police what you did to me." I stepped closer to the bed.

The doctors were able to repair the damage from the bullet. Alton was still weak from surgery but just as determined as ever. He scoffed. Angling his face away from me. "What I did to you? I'm the one in the hospital. Look at you. You look fine to me."

"You terrorized and drugged me. God knows what else you were planning." I didn't even want to imagine how that night could've ended for me.

He let out a dry, wheezing laugh. "What I was planning? None of this was me. I was only taking orders. How are you so stupid that you still don't understand?"

"Explain it to me then. What is Raoul?"

He shook his head and looked at me with pity. "Does it matter? He was going to share his gift with me. That's all I cared about."

"You mean the gift of living forever?" My voice wavered with the question because I was still unsure. It was such an impossibility.

"Yeah." He looked at the door. "He could give me eternal life."

"Did he?"

He scowled. "What do you think?"

I watched him as I stood chewing on my lip. "What was he?"

Alton looked into my eyes. "He is life itself."

"Don't you mean was," I quipped.

A slow smile spread across his face. "Was."

He hadn't answered my question, but I doubted he really had an answer. "What did he want with me?" I was looking for an answer I already had buried deep within myself.

"How should I know? I just promised to give him what he wanted in exchange for what I wanted."

"And your grandmother?" I thought of the pain in Glory's face after she pulled the trigger.

"She didn't know anything. I told her you were hexed." The hard edge to his voice gave me chills. He'd fooled us all.

"It was all you from the beginning." I felt so stupid. How hadn't I realized that Alton was the one trying so desperately to think I was hexed?

He smirked. "When I sent you that flyer about the house, I knew you would bite. Raoul said you were conditioned to be drawn to that house. I guess he was right."

"And the graffiti and the hex?" I was searching for confirmation to put my mind at ease.

"All me. Raoul told me what to do sometimes, but mostly I impro-vised." He waved his fingers close to his body as if revealing a magic trick. "When I first met him, I had no idea who he was. He was just another client looking for a quiet place in the country. As we walked through a little ranch house on the edge of town, I started to get a strange vibe from him. He wasn't like anyone I'd ever met before. He dressed and spoke like someone from another time. I wasn't familiar with his artwork before, so I didn't recognize him. After showing him a few houses over the course of several weeks, he came clean with me. He told me that he wasn't really interested in buying a house, but he did want me to do him a favor. I'm no idiot. I thought he must have some kind of scam up his sleeve, so I blew him off, but he wouldn't leave me alone. Eventually, I decided to hear him out. His story was outrageous. He told me that he could help me win the race against time if I could help him get hold of you. I'm a goal-oriented guy. Yeah, I've achieved a lot in life, but there was so much more I wanted to achieve. I often feel like time is slipping through my fingers. The years pass so quickly now. How will I ever see everything I want to see? Do everything I want to do? So, when he began to hint that there was a way of prolonging my life, I found the offer appealing. In the beginning, I wasn't quite sure if I believed him, but..." he pressed his lips together and blinked slowly, "he's charismatic. He has a way of making you believe the impossible, and the more time I spent with him, the more I felt compelled to do whatever he asked me to do."

"But you did realize he wasn't human." A flash of what his face had become shot into my memory.

Alton looked at me with a confused expression. "Does it matter?"

"Of course it does."

He blinked at me blankly.

"The way his face changed at the house; didn't it terrify you?"

Alton shook his head. "I've seen a lot of terrible things in my life-time."

The way he looked at me made me doubt myself. Maybe Raoul's face hadn't changed at all. Alton was acting like nothing notable had happened. Did I really see tentacles coming out of Raoul's head? "You saw it, right? You saw the way his face melted off?"

Alton suddenly looked exhausted. He blinked slowly. "Are you here for a reason?"

Doubt flooded my thoughts. Maybe whatever it was that Glory gave me had made me hallucinate. I sighed. Pressing him on this point felt useless. "So, he didn't tell you what he was going to do to me?"

Alton shook his head. "He said that he needed to do a ceremony that would bind you two together forever so you would never leave him again. All I had to do was make sure you showed up, and he would do the rest, so that's what I did." His eyelids drooped.

"You never once thought that you might be putting me in danger?" I watched his face, looking for a hint of regret, but saw none.

He closed his eyes too long to be a blink. When he opened them again, his gaze was unfocused. "You are no one to me, so I didn't care."

The words stung. I hated to think people could be so uncaring to one another. Even though I hadn't gotten the answers I was looking for I couldn't be in the room with him any longer. I left without another word.

CHAPTER 24

When we pulled up to the Valley Inn, Mr. Xavier was standing on the front porch.

"I can't believe you want to come back here. I could've picked up your stuff for you." Davida put her truck into park.

I looked out the window. "I need to talk to him. Maybe he can answer some questions."

Davida looked at Mr. Xavier, who raised his coffee cup at us in acknowledgment. "I know he saved you, but I don't trust him." She turned off the car and reached for the door handle.

"I think I should do this alone." I placed my hand on her arm, hoping she wouldn't be offended. "You don't mind, do you?" I hadn't told her about everything.

"I'll wait here." She was still watching Mr. Xavier when I got out of the truck.

"Are you all right?" he asked as I approached the porch. This man, whom I'd seen as a suspicious oddball, had become a protector to me.

"Yeah, I'm okay, considering." We hadn't talked much since the incident, but I wanted answers and found that Alton couldn't give them. I wondered if Mr. Xavier could. "What were you doing out at Warner Manor that night?"

He looked toward the tree line. Then he took a slow sip of his coffee. "Why don't we go inside and talk?" He went to the door and held it open, waiting for me. We sat at the bar in the kitchen. The bed and breakfast was quiet. I wondered where Mrs. Xavier was but didn't ask. Instead, I sat on the hard wooden barstool in the kitchen while Mr. Xavier poured me a cup of coffee. I'd been there so long now that he already knew that I liked it with a little bit of cream and a heaping teaspoon of sugar. He sat it on the bar in front of me.

"Wait here. I want to show you something." He disappeared into the room off the kitchen. I'd seen them go back there many times before. I assumed it was their office. I heard him moving around, possibly opening and closing a cabinet door before reappearing. He sat a plastic file box in front of me. Looking through it, he pulled out some photos and put them in front of me next to my coffee cup. "Raoul Bonnaire, as he calls himself, has been kicking around this town for many years. You see this picture." He jabbed his finger at the photo in front of me. "That's my father with Raoul, but he wasn't Raoul at the time."

"What do you mean?" I leaned down to get a closer look at the picture.

"He was Michael Turner back then. My father told me he'd asked him to help lure a woman into town for him. He had a very specific woman in mind. My father started to help him but changed his mind. He said something didn't seem right. Later, the woman died—suicide. My father didn't believe it."

"He didn't believe it was a suicide?" I asked.

He shook his head. "No. Something wasn't right. So, he started following Raoul. He told me he saw things he couldn't explain. He'd watched him go out into the woods and walk down into the lake. The first time he saw him do it, he thought he was killing himself, but he didn't. He walked right out into the water clear over his head. My father said he stayed there for ages, watching and waiting to see him float to the top, but he didn't resurface for an hour. Then he walked right back up out, his skin glistening like scales in the moonlight. My father said he wasn't a man, but he was something else, something dangerous."

"Like what? A sea creature?" I remembered how he looked to me when his face melted away. Even though I didn't know if it had really happened, the image was still so clear.

He nodded. "He sure did look like one."

Relief washed over me. "You saw it too? You saw his face melt away?"

"How could I miss it?" He shook his head. "I'll never forget it. I still see it in my nightmares."

A tear stung the corner of my eye. "Me too."

"Back then, my father told the other townspeople what he saw, but nobody believed him. So, he decided to confront him about what he'd seen. Raoul told him that he was seeing things. He told him to stop drinking so much moonshine. My father didn't drink. He knew what he saw. So, he just continued to watch him. That's when he found out he wasn't the only one like him around. There were others. They would all gather together at the lake. They'd walk into the water together and walk out again hours later. No human being can hold their breath for that long." He looked at me when he said that as if to gauge my reaction.

"How many were there?"

He shrugged. "He told me that I saw seven all together." He paused. "He wasn't the only one who saw something strange by the lake. I saw them too. I saw a lot of things that summer, but I was a kid. I convinced myself that I had imagined it all up until my father told me about it many years later."

"And they all lived here?"

He shook his head. "No. He'd never seen the others before. He didn't know where they came from."

"But what would they want with me?"

"I'm not sure, but he was always looking for women." He cleared his throat. I should say that he was always looking for a specific woman.

"What do you mean?"

He pulled a picture from the box and handed it to me. In it, Raoul held hands with a woman who seemed familiar to me. "As soon as I saw you, I knew you were one of them. When you told me about the numbers appearing on the mirror, I knew for sure."

"Then why did you act like you thought I was some kind of lunatic?" I remembered how unwelcome he made me feel.

"Because I wanted you to leave. I thought if you got far away from this town, nothing would happen to you."

"Why didn't you just tell me?" My voice cracked.

"That Raoul Bonnaire is a monster who lives forever and will probably make you kill yourself? You never would've believed that."

He was right. I wouldn't have.

"I hadn't seen him around since he'd disappeared. I'd thought that he'd ruined any chance at anonymity by making himself into a star in the seventies. I'd hoped he'd given up and returned to wherever he came from. Then you showed up, and I knew he was back. If he was back, that would mean you wouldn't last long. Every woman he brought here ended up dead, eventually."

"Do you know why?"

"I don't, but don't you think you might kill yourself if you discovered that the man you loved was really a monster?"

I thought about this idea for a moment. "No, I wouldn't."

"Don't be so sure."

"Do you think he's dead?"

Mr. Xavier shook his head. "Nothing can kill him. He always comes back here eventually. That's why you need to get out of here as soon as possible and never come back."

"I was already planning that."

"Good."

"But what if he tries to find me again?" There was no way I could convince myself that escaping Raoul would be as easy as leaving town.

Mr. Xavier picked up the picture he'd placed in front of me and looked at it before placing it back in his folder. "If you leave before he resurrects himself, I'm willing to bet you'll be in the clear for a little while."

I wasn't so sure about that. I took a long sip of my coffee, which had grown cool while we talked. I got up from my stool with it in my hand. "My friend is waiting for me outside. I should hurry and get my stuff."

"Yes, you should."

CHAPTER 25

D avida wasn't surprised when I told her to scrap the project. We sold the house as is to an overseas investor. Even though we lost money, I'm sure she was as happy as I was to get out of that town. We fell back into our normal lives easily. I bought a place in the city, a small brownstone to flip. It was the kind of project I did early in my career. I'd had big plans for Warner Manor but plans change.

Even though I tried to act like everything was normal, I couldn't forget what had happened. Sometimes, I had nightmares about Raoul. I couldn't get the image of his face melting away out of my mind. The creature he'd become right in front of me haunted my thoughts. Sometimes, I'd wake up in the middle of the night with the distinct feeling that someone was watching me. In the darkness of my apartment, I would mistake a coat hanging on the back of a chair for a person sitting there. My life had become a series of false scares.

Eager to have a nice night out, I went to an art opening to see the work of an artist from Florida. Art patrons packed into the gallery space, enthusiastic about this new young talent. Excitement charged the air. As I walked among the crowd with my glass of chardonnay, I kept thinking I saw Raoul watching me from across the room. I hurried toward the man on the other side of the room who looked like him, weaving through the people until I got to the place where I thought he was. He wasn't there. Still, the idea of Raoul haunted me. I spun around in a circle, doing my best to look over the crowd, but I didn't see him.

No one could blame me for being paranoid since that night at Warner Manor. I was always looking over my shoulder. I constantly thought I caught sight of Raoul sitting in a cafe window, in the crush of people on the subway, or passing me on the street on a bike. Whenever I would crane my neck to get a better look, it was never him, and I'd have a couple of moments to relax before my paranoia would kick into high gear again.

I was taking a few deep breaths to calm my nerves when a tawny man walked up to me. He was handsome, and I'd talked to him before but was having trouble pulling his name from the murky depths of my mind. "Are you okay?" he asked, putting his hand on the small of my back.

Flustered, I looked at him. "Michael? Is that right?"

He smiled at me. "Yes, Khadijah."

"I'm feeling a little out of sorts. How are you doing?"

He began to talk, and I was happy to hear about his life, his career, his friends, and his family. The conversation was so normal that I wanted to jump inside of it and let it take me away from everything in my strange life. I was completely engrossed when one of the waiters came up to me and handed me a folded cocktail napkin. "A gentleman asked me to give this to you." He wore a devilish smile as he passed the napkin to me.

Michael stopped talking; an annoyed look passed over his face.

I glanced around. "Who?" I asked.

"He was right over there." The waiter turned and gestured across the room. Then he looked around, confused. "I don't see him now, but he was right over there."

I unfolded the napkin to see the number eight written again and again in blue ink. "What's that?" Michael asked, looking at it over my shoulder.

I shook my head and swallowed the lump in my throat. My pulse raced. I *had* seen him. "Nothing," I croaked. I stood on my tiptoes, looking over the crowd, but I didn't see him anywhere. I didn't have to see him to know he was there. I was right. I was being watched.

CHAPTER 26

My whole body began to shake with fear, and I wondered if my legs would give out. I grabbed hold of Michael's arm to steady me.

"Are you okay? Do you need to sit down?" Michael put his hand on the small of my back and looked around the room. "Come with me." He steered me toward a bench against the wall only a few feet from where we stood.

I lowered myself to sit, grateful to get off my feet before I passed out. Gripping the edge of the cold, smooth wood, I took a few deep breaths. Ever since I came back to the city, I felt like something was wrong. Davida had told me that it was only natural considering what I had been through, but my instincts told me it was something more. Now my instincts were proving to be right.

Michael came through the crowd, holding a small water bottle. I hadn't even noticed that he'd left. He sat down on the bench next to me. "Here you go." He handed me the bottle. "Feeling any better?"

It was shockingly cold in my hand. I opened it and took a swig even though I knew it wouldn't help.

"There must've been something pretty terrible written on that napkin." He looked down at the folded napkin in my lap before raising his gaze to meet mine.

I shook my head. How could I explain what I still couldn't believe myself? What I'd seen at Warner Manor affected me deeply, haunting my dreams and terrorizing my waking hours. I gripped the napkin in my hand and twisted it into a ball. "It's nothing. Just a message from someone I used to know."

"I assume it wasn't a good message." His eyes held mine, searching.

I shook my head. "I'm not really in the art opening mood anymore." I stood, still feeling a little unsteady on my feet. "I think I'll head home."

Michael got up too. "I'll help you get a cab."

Normally, I would have turned down his offer, but I was so scared that I let him accompany me outside.

Cars jammed the streets, but there wasn't a taxi in sight. Michael stood in front of me, looking down the road at the stream of oncoming headlights. "It's been good getting reacquainted." He pulled his hand from his pocket and handed me a business card. "I'd love to see you again. You can call me any time."

I took the card. "Thanks," I said weakly. Spotting an empty cab coming our way, I raised my hand in the air and stepped confidently toward the curb. It weaved through traffic and pulled up in front of me. Michael was fast to reach over and open the door.

"You'll call me?" His face was uncomfortably close to mine.

I gave a curt nod and tried my best to smile. "Of course." I slid into the taxi before he could say anything else to me. Sitting in the back of the cab, I remembered I still had the balled-up napkin in my hand. I smoothed it out on my lap. It was too dark to see what was written on the white square of paper, but I didn't have to see it again to feel the dread creeping through me as the taxi bumped along the busy streets. It was just a single number, but it brought up so much fear in me.

I checked the time. It was eight-thirty, which meant it wasn't too late to call Davida. I pulled my phone from my purse and dialed her number. She picked up right away.

"How's the art opening?" I could hear the television blaring in the background. One of her sons talked loudly over the noise. The buzz of activity in her house faded, and I pictured her slipping away into another room.

"I'm heading home." I stared out of the window at the lit-up store-fronts passing by.

"It's early."

"Something crazy happened to me." Tears pricked the back of my eyes, and emotions swelled in me. I cleared my throat. "Someone gave the waiter a note for me. It was the number eight. That's it. Just the number eight written on a napkin."

Davida gasped. "Who gave it to you?"

"The waiter, but I don't know who gave it to him. I didn't see anyone. When I asked him, he pointed to the other side of the room, but he said the person was gone."

"Did you find out what he looked like?" Urgency filled her voice.

"No. I was so freaked out that I just wanted to get out of there." I should've asked the waiter more questions.

"Where are you now?"

"In a taxi on my way home." I looked out the window as the cab rolled through the streets.

"It's probably nothing." The unusually high pitch of her voice betrayed her doubts.

"How could it be nothing? Someone is obviously watching me." Even as I sat in the taxi, I could feel eyes on me. I glanced toward the driver, who slouched in his seat with one hand resting casually on the top of the steering wheel. He was a round-faced man. Dark stubble dabbled his cheeks. He only talked to me when I got into the cab to find out where I was going. After that, he was silent.

"Maybe you should come here and stay in the guest room. Just to be safe."

"I'm sure it'll be fine. I'm already home." The taxi glided to a stop in front of my building. Staying at Davida's house would've been nice. She had always taken good care of me, but I was an adult who needed to face these things on my own. I didn't want to get her family involved in whatever this was. What happened at Warner Manor had broken what I'd previously known as reality, but I was determined to reclaim it. "Don't worry about me. I'll be fine. I'll call you tomorrow."

"Okay. You're always welcome to come here. Call me if you need anything."

"I will."

As the taxi drove away, I realized how empty the street was. I was utterly alone. The streetlight immediately in front of my place was out. It had been that way for a while now. The branches of the nearby maple tree stretched into the sky, casting sinister shadows on the sidewalk. I hurried up my front stairs, searching my purse for my key and quietly cursing myself for not retrieving them before getting out of the cab. Finally, I found them. Just as I stuck the key in the lock, someone behind me said my name. I froze, the hairs on the back of my neck standing on end.

"Khadijah," the voice was firm and familiar.

Slowly, I turned to see Officer Moses standing there. He looked different when he wasn't wearing his uniform. He wore a black jacket over a Yankees t-shirt and dark-wash jeans.

"Officer Moses?" He was the last person I expected to see.

"Devin," he said. "I'm technically off-duty."

I nodded.

"Do you have a minute? I need to talk to you." He took a few steps closer to me but did not climb the stairs.

I crossed my arms over my chest. "Okay. Go on and talk then."

He frowned. "Could I come inside, or maybe there's someplace we could go?" He looked up the dark, empty street.

"I don't see why we can't talk right here," I added a hardness to my voice.

He pressed his lips together and looked at his feet before walking up the staircase toward me. My whole body tensed. Could the napkin have come from him? I held it out in front of him. "You sent this to me, didn't you?"

He stopped three steps away from me. Confusion crossed his face. "Why would I send you a balled-up napkin?"

Frazzled, I smooth it out to reveal the eight written on it. "Someone just sent this to me at an art opening. It's just like what they were writing on the manor's walls to scare me away."

"I don't have anything to do with that." He nodded toward the napkin.

I didn't know if I should believe him or not. "Why are you here then? How did you find me?"

"You're not exactly hard to track down." He drew his eyebrows together. "I'm not here to play games. I'm here to get some questions answered. What everyone says happened at the manor that night doesn't add up, so I'd like to get your version of the events again."

Even though I hadn't done anything wrong, I felt the sweat gathering in my armpits. My heart thumped in my chest. "Why don't you ask your buddy Alton what happened?" I don't know why I said that. I knew that if any of us changed our story, Alton would be the one to do it.

"That's part of the problem. I can't ask Alton anything because he disappeared once he got out of the hospital."

"What do you mean he disappeared?" He was seriously injured. I didn't see how he could have the capacity to disappear.

"Just what I said. He's gone. No one has seen him. He hasn't shown up to any of his physical therapy appointments. He checked out of the hospital and vanished." He narrowed his eyes at me like he thought I had something to do with it.

"I haven't seen him." I looked at the napkin still in my hand. "Unless..."

His gaze drifted to the napkin and then back to me. "What are you implying?"

"Unless he's the one who sent me this."

"Why would he do that?" The edge in his voice suggested that he didn't appreciate the accusation. I'd forgotten that he had no idea about his friend's involvement in what happened to me. In his world, the only thing terrible that happened that night in the manor was Alton getting shot. He didn't see the horrible monster that I saw. He didn't know that Alton was trying to sacrifice me to it, or at least that's what I thought he was trying to do. He didn't know any of it. To him, I could've been the bad guy.

"I don't know. Your guess is as good as mine. I only know that somebody is following me."

"You've seen someone following you?"

I shrugged. "Not exactly, but there is this."

He shook his head. "Anyone could've sent you that."

"It is obvious that whoever sent it knew about what happened."

"It could've been a coincidence." I hated how those words sounded so reasonable as they rolled off his tongue.

"What kind of coincidence would this be? Who sends someone a number eight on a napkin?" I was unwilling to concede. He was wrong, and no matter how insane I seemed to him, I wouldn't let him think he was right, not even for a moment.

He frowned. "I'm not here to talk about a napkin. I'm here to find out what you know about Alton. Do you know where he is?" His dark eyes burrowed into me.

I shook my head. "Why would I know where he is?" I hadn't heard from Alton since I saw him in the hospital.

Officer Moses grimaced. "Okay then, if that's the story you're going with." He sighed, and his posture softened a bit. Then he turned to walk away from me.

"That's the story I'm going with because it's the truth." Frustration roiled inside of me. I wanted to tell him everything. "You didn't have to come all this way to ask me that. You could've just picked up the phone." I called after him as he walked away from me.

He turned back to look at me, amusement registering on his face. "Why do you think you're the only reason I have to come to the city?" He smirked. "Have a good night, Khadijah."

"You too." I watched him walk up the sidewalk and disappear into the darkness. I stood on my porch holding the napkin with the figure eight in my hand. When I realized that I was completely and utterly alone again and someone might be watching me, I slid my key into the lock and hurried inside to the safety of my home.

CHapTer 27

When I turned on the light, all of my belongings appeared as they should have, but still, I felt like something was terribly wrong. Goosebumps rose on my arms, and I focused all my energy on listening. Had someone been in my house? Were they still there? I stood still, illuminated by the globe pendant in my entryway. Every cell in my body was trained on listening. There was only silence.

"Calm down," I whispered to myself. I took a deep breath before sliding out of my black high heels. I flipped the switch on the wall to my right, and the overhead light in the living room came to life, flooding the dark corners with a bright white glow. I cocked my head, my ears straining to pick out any unusual sounds.

"If there is anyone here, I want you to know that I am armed," I called into the empty space, hoping my voice landed on no one's ears.

I padded into the living room. The soft shag of my rug met my bare feet. I moved through the house methodically, checking every dark corner, looking for evidence someone had been there. Only when I was sure I was alone did I even consider going to bed. First, I had to call Davida and tell her I was okay.

She answered right away. "Are you safe and sound?"

"Yeah, but you'll never guess who was standing on my doorstep when I got here."

"Who?" she asked.

"Officer Moses."

"From Farrington?" She was just as confused by this turn of events as I was.

"Yeah. He told me that Alton disappeared when he got released from the hospital, and he thinks I've got something to do with it." The sharp edge of anger crept into my voice.

"What? How could he accuse you of anything like that? You should've had him and his raggedy grandmother arrested," she hissed.

"Glory didn't know anything about his plans. She was trying to help." I felt sympathy for Glory. Her own grandson had tricked her. I couldn't imagine the heartbreak she must've felt when she realized the truth.

"I don't know about that. I don't see how she couldn't have known something fishy was going on. They drugged you." Davida didn't know what had really happened in Warner Manor that night. No one who wasn't there did.

"Relatives know your blind spots best. Of course, he was able to trick her." I remembered how much I liked Alton when I first met him. He was good-looking, charming, and helpful. I had no clue about his sinister intentions.

"She was blinded by love, in a sense," Davida said.

"Exactly." I was blinded by infatuation, but I didn't want to admit that to anyone, not even Davida.

"Well, it's pretty obvious who gave you the note then."

"I know what you're thinking, but I'm not so sure." I thought of how confused Officer Moses seemed when I showed him that note. "Officer Moses wasn't involved in anything back in Farrington."

"How do you know that?" she asked.

"I just have a feeling."

"Feelings can be wrong. You know that." Someone yelled in the background. Davida gave a muffled response. I imagined her in her home office with her hand over the receiver, calling out to one of her boys.

"I know from experience. I should've learned my lesson by now." I wanted to think of myself as street-smart, but I'd been conned more than a few times in life.

"Yeah, you should've." I heard a boy's voice shrieking.

"Sounds like you're needed." I yawned. "I'll let you go. I'm exhausted. I need to get some sleep."

"You're not the only one." She sighed.

After hanging up, I sat on the sofa for a few minutes, staring at the napkin and thinking until my eyelids grew heavy with sleep. I was grateful to be able to slip off into dreamland without the help of any pharmaceuticals. Ever since that night, I'd been unable to sleep on my own. Every time I closed my eyes, I saw Raoul's face melting away, the skin bubbling, oozing, and sliding down to reveal something beyond my comprehension. Drugs took all those images away, yanking me into a dark, empty sleep devoid of color. That was the kind of sleep I slipped into naturally that night. It was the only kind of sleep that let me feel even the slightest bit rested.

At midnight, I woke with a start from a nightmare. In it, I was at the art opening again, talking to Michael, when I got the note. It was just like what had happened in real life, but in my dream, I found Raoul in the gallery. He was leaving, and I caught up to him just outside the door. When I called his name, he turned around, and his face burst open, the skin splitting like a rubber mask. Red tentacles spilled from his flesh, glistening with translucent slime. One reached for me. It wound its way around my neck, warm and slick.

I sat up. My breath was ragged as I turned on the bedside lamp and searched the room with my eyes. It was a nightmare. I'd had many since that night, but this one felt so real. A chill shot through me, and I had the distinct feeling someone was watching me. I got out of bed and searched the house again for a sign of an intruder. There was no one there. Now, with all the lights on and adrenaline coursing through my veins, I knew I would not be able to get back to sleep on my own. So I turned off all the lights, retrieved the amber pill bottle from the drawer at my bedside, and took one of the tiny pink pills, confident it would propel me into a deep, dark, dreamless sleep.

I awoke in the morning groggy and not quite ready to face the day. A column of light came through the crack in my cream-colored curtains. I groaned and pulled the sheet over my head. I couldn't stay in bed forever. I had to get up and get some work done. I had to act like everything in my life was normal, even though I knew it would never be normal again.

I sighed as I pulled the sheet off. Sitting up, I noticed something unusual sitting on the table beside my bed. A newspaper lay open. Fear tore through me. My body began to shake. I didn't have to look at it. I grabbed hold of the edge of the paper as if touching it would bring me great harm and cautiously pulled it into my lap. The paper had been carefully folded so a specific picture looked up at me. Even though I'd seen it before, the sight of it turned my blood to ice.

My own face stared back at me from the page, wearing the same dark dress I'd found buried in the ground. I took a few deep, wheezing breaths. How was this happening? No matter how badly I wanted to put everything behind me, I couldn't. Whoever was out there doing all of this wouldn't let me.

I jumped when my phone dinged on the bedside table. I grabbed it, hoping it would be a message from Davida. When I opened the text message, I saw a single eight. The text came from a number I didn't recognize. Without thinking, I pressed call and dialed it. As I listened to it ring, my fear transformed into fury. How could anyone think they had the right to keep me in a constant state of fear? They'd traumatized me so much that I didn't know what was real anymore. The phone rang, and with every ring, I got angrier and angrier. It rang and rang and rang, and no one picked up. No voice recording came on, telling me to leave a message. It kept ringing. Then I heard a click, and the line went silent.

"Hello," I said into the phone. "Is anybody there?"

Silence answered me.

"Leave me alone," I yelled into the phone before hanging up. I sat with the phone in my lap and my heart pounding. Still not satisfied, I decided to text the number.

"Who are you?"

I watched as the dots in the text box flickered to life. Someone was typing an answer. They moved back and forth for what felt like an eternity. I sat glued to the screen, waiting for their reply.

I was disappointed when their response appeared. "You already know," the text said.

I hit the green call button again. I would make whoever was behind this talk to me. The phone rang in my ear three times. Then I heard a click, and the line went silent again. I held the phone away from my ear and looked at it incredulously. Then I hit the green button again. This time, it only rang once before someone answered.

"Who is this?" I asked.

Even though the person on the other end of the line didn't speak, I knew they were there. I felt their presence pressing into me through the phone.

"Who is this?" I tried desperately to mask the fear in my voice, but it still trembled.

Silence answered me.

"If you don't stop harassing me, I'll call the police."

Again, no one answered, but they were still on the line. I could hear the whisper of their breath.

"Officer Devin Moses?" I waited again for an answer, hoping saying someone's name would move them to speak. "Or is this Alton?"

The silence on the other end of the line grew heavy. It was almost like a living, breathing creature that could slip out the phone and slowly encompass me. I swallowed the lump in my throat.

"Raoul?" I whispered. Merely saying his name turned my stomach.

Again, there was no answer, but the shift in the air around me told me I was right.

"Raoul?" I repeated his name, like acid on my tongue. Then I waited for an answer. Instead of the usual silence, I heard the click of whoever was on the other end of the call hanging up. I lowered the phone from my ear. With a few taps, I brought the text message back up and reread it.

"You already know."

CHAPTER 28

A fter that phone call, I wanted to talk to Davida again, but I knew her mornings were busy. So, I picked up my phone and called someone else. He answered after the first ring.

"I thought your generation only sent text messages," Douglas Xavier said into the phone. His voice had a lightness that I'd only gotten to know since I left Farrington.

"Sometimes we make phone calls too." I paused, the weight of what I was about to say heavy in my thoughts. I didn't want to explain this to him, but he was one of the few people who would understand and believe me.

"Well, it's good to hear your voice. Are you doing well?" He waited for my answer.

I suspected the question was an attempt to pull whatever I needed to say out of me. He knew I wouldn't call, not unless something was wrong. "You'll never guess who showed up on my doorstep last night."

"Devin Moses," he said his name flatly.

"How did you know?"

"I didn't really, but why else would you call? I knew he was going to the city. He supposedly has friends to see there, but I think he's on the hunt for Alton."

"Wait a minute, Doug." We were on a first-name basis now. It was natural after all that we had seen. "You knew he was coming here and didn't tell me." I held my hand up like he could see me as I realized something else he'd said. "And you knew Alton was missing and didn't tell me that either!"

"I thought it was best if you had some time to recover and process what happened." He spoke sternly, even though his intentions were kind. "I didn't think Moses would show up on your doorstep."

"Well, he did. He thinks I know something about Alton?"

"Do you?" he asked.

I scowled. I couldn't believe he was asking me that. "I just told you that I didn't know he was missing. I've been trying to forget everything that happened up there." I paused. Whenever I mentioned Farrington, that horrible image of Raoul's face splitting open came to mind. I shook the dreadful thought off before continuing. "How long has he been gone?"

Doug sighed. "Maybe a couple of weeks now. He disappeared as soon as they released him from the hospital."

I wanted him to say more. "No one's heard anything from him?"

"No, but hopefully, he's learned his lesson. He was messing around with a dark force, and nothing good ever comes from that." Birds chirped in the background. I imagined Doug sitting on the large front porch at Valley Inn with a cup of coffee. "Things have been quiet here, but I don't think it will last."

"What do you mean?" I closed my eyes. My eyelids were heavy with fatigue.

"You can't kill something that's lived for as long as Raoul has as easily as that. I think he's just laying low. Maybe he needs to recover, and he'll be back." Even though Doug had been following Raoul for much of his life, not even he was prepared for the revelation of what Raoul truly was. I wondered if it had broken his brain like it seemed to have broken mine. I smoothed the newspaper out in front of me and examined the grainy picture of someone who looked exactly like me from a time long before I was even thought of. "He's already back." The words seemed to suck all of the moisture out of my mouth. I cleared my throat.

"What do you mean?"

"When I woke up this morning, one of the old newspapers from Warner Manor was on my nightstand. There's a picture of a woman who looks just like me in it." I couldn't look at the picture any longer, so I raised my gaze to the wall, a tear slipping down my cheek. I was glad Doug couldn't see me. I wiped the tear away and did my best to bundle up my emotions so he wouldn't hear them in my voice. "I went out to an art opening the other night. It was the first time I'd done anything like that in ages because..." I didn't have to finish the sentence he already knew. "Anyway, someone gave the waiter a napkin to give me with a figure eight drawn on it."

"Who?"

"I don't know. The waiter said someone asked him to give it to me. When we looked around, the person was gone."

"And someone broke into your house and put a newspaper on the nightstand?"

He had said the obvious, but hearing him suggest that someone had gotten into the house while I slept made my heart start thumping again. I still hadn't gotten up from bed. For all I knew, someone was still in the house. I swallowed the lump in my throat.

"How did they get in?"

"I don't know. Everything was locked." As I spoke, I slid out of bed and began checking around the house again. In the past few months, I had made checking to see if everything was locked such a ritual that I felt like I was developing OCD. Everything was locked up tight. "There was no way anyone could have gotten in unless they had a key. How would that be?"

"Does someone have an extra key?"

His question startled me. I wasn't even aware that I'd been saying that part aloud. "That would be impossible."

"Who have you given an extra key to?" He was determined to solve this mystery on the phone right now.

"Nobody ... I mean, just Davida, but she wouldn't have given it to anyone else."

There was a long pause. "I want you to come back here and stay at the inn for a while. This obviously isn't over, and I'd feel better with you nearby. Raoul is after you, and we need to figure this out together. I don't like you staying there alone. It's not safe."

"People got into my room there too, remember?"

"I know," he said, "but if you're here, we can work together and figure this out."

I sighed. I knew I should welcome his help, but I couldn't face going back to where this all started. "Maybe it's not for you to figure out. He's after me, and I think I'm the only one who can do something about it."

"I know that's what you think, but that's not true. He might be after you, but his existence affects all of us. He's not the only one." He lowered his voice as if sharing a secret with me.

"How?"

He cleared his throat. "I'd rather tell you in person."

I smiled. He didn't realize how stubborn I was yet. "That's not going to happen unless you plan a city trip."

"I'm a small-town guy."

I sucked my teeth. "That's unfortunate because I'm not going to Farrington again anytime soon, not if I can avoid it. Davida will let me stay at her house again. Nothing weird happened when I stayed with her before. Maybe I should just do that for a little while."

"You do that for now, but it won't solve anything." I could hear the muffled sound of him talking to someone. "I have to go."

"Okay."

"I will call you later." He covered the phone, and I could hear more muffled conversation. "I have to go," he said into the phone again. "Khadijah, Be careful." The words hung on the line, and I knew there was so much more he wanted to say but couldn't.

"Don't worry. I will," I said before hanging up.

I never thought I'd be in therapy, but ever since that night, I felt I had no choice. I knew I'd lose my mind if I didn't try to talk to someone about what happened. Naturally, I left a lot out. I had to. The details didn't matter as much as how it made me feel. I only told Dr. Montague what she needed to know to help me, and I looked forward to going to her office every week to talk.

I settled into the soft navy blue chair that seemed to wrap around me like a hug. Dr. Montague sat across from me with her legs crossed. Her gray-streaked chestnut brown hair was swept into a side ponytail. She waited for me to begin talking, but now that I was here, I wasn't sure what to say. I cleared my throat and looked at my lap. I'd thrown on the first pair of jeans I saw that morning and didn't realize until I was out that a coffee stain marred the right thigh. I swore every time I looked down at it that it got bigger. I used to be so put together. There was a time when I'd never leave the house in stained jeans or with my hair in a frizzy ponytail. My clothes were always pressed, and my edges were always laid, but not anymore. I was coming undone, and it felt like everyone could see it.

"Well?" Dr. Montague said. She was usually good at waiting for me to speak, but we had been sitting in silence for a while now.

Tears pricked the back of my eyes. I blinked, hoping to keep them from flowing. I knew it was okay to fall apart here, but the flood of emotions that washed over me took me by surprise. I cleared my throat and began to talk. Tears flowed as I told her about the note and Officer Moses.

She stopped me mid-story, holding up her hand. "The person who drugged you wasn't arrested?"

I shook my head. "I thought getting shot was punishment enough."

She frowned, just like everyone else I knew had when I told them, but they didn't understand how complicated it was. "He's probably stalking you. It is not unreasonable to think that he has found you again and intends to finish what he started."

"I don't think he will. I don't think he can." My real concern was much bigger than anything Alton could do.

Dr. Montague shook her head. "I can't make you do anything, but not reporting this to the police is unwise." She pursed her lips and drew her eyebrows together. "And this Officer Moses person isn't interested in arresting his friend for breaking the law?"

"He doesn't know." I wondered what he would do if he did know.

She shook her head. "This is very serious. You are in danger."

I pressed my lips together. I wished I could tell her everything. Maybe then she'd understand. "Alton won't do anything to me."

"You can't know that." She sat forward in her chair, and I felt the energy in the room shift. She wasn't just talking to me as a therapist now. She was concerned.

"It's going to be okay." I hoped that just saying it would make it true. I dried my eyes with a tissue. "I'm just shaken up a bit because I thought it was all over, and this caught me off guard. It's going to work out though." I didn't know that. No one could. I didn't even believe it, but maybe if I started to say it, it would be true.

"How?" She tilted her head.

I shrugged. "It just will."

CHAPTER 29

I called Davida. Doug was right. I couldn't stay in my condo alone. Even if I tried, I didn't think I'd be able to sleep, so I went to her house.

Davida greeted me with a smile. "Come on in." She gave me a hug, and I nearly started to cry again.

"Hi, Auntie." Davida's youngest rushed through the room and into the kitchen, where he flung the refrigerator open.

"No snacks. We're eating dinner soon," she called to him.

"But I'm hungry now." He leaned over, looking into the refrigerator.

"You're not going to starve." Davida put her hands on her hips. "Close the door."

He shut the refrigerator door so hard the bottles of condiments rattled inside.

"Don't try me." She wagged her finger at him.

"Sorry," he mumbled before hurrying out of the room and up the stairs.

"These boys. I swear." Davida shook her head. "Dinner isn't much. I didn't have time to cook, so I was just heating up leftovers."

"I don't mind leftovers, but I might skip dinner. I don't have much of an appetite these days anyway." My stomach gargled as if disagreeing with me, and I placed my arm over my midriff.

Davida smirked. "Well, if you change your mind, we have plenty of food."

I ended up eating dinner after all. When I saw that one of the leftover choices was lasagna, I couldn't refuse. The leftover lasagna was perfect. As usual, I loved sitting around the table with Davida's family. They always made me feel like I was one of them. It was exactly what I needed to calm down. Her sons' playful banter during dinner almost made me forget why I was there. I couldn't forget for long though. Nothing in my life was normal anymore, no matter how badly I wanted it to be.

"Have you talked to the police?" Davida's husband asked me as I helped put away the dishes after dinner.

I frowned. "About what?"

"I don't know everything that's going on. Davida has not exactly been forthcoming." He slid his gaze over to his wife, who was wiping the counter. "But from what I've heard, I'm pretty sure this is a matter for the police. Someone has been breaking into your house, is that right?"

I nodded slowly. "I think so."

"You think so." He raised an eyebrow at me.

I nodded. "It's complicated." The white plate in my hand felt unusually heavy. "I'm just going to be here for a few nights."

He sighed. "Don't get me wrong, Khadijah. You're always welcome here, but I want to make sure you're safe. When someone breaks into your house, you call the police."

"I know you're trying to help, but I have to deal with this my own way."

He opened his mouth to say something else, but Davida nudged him in the ribs.

"Don't worry about it, baby. We're taking care of it." Davida glanced at me. "Aren't we?"

I nodded. "There's already a cop involved," I added. "He came by last night."

Davida narrowed her eyes at me but didn't say anything more.

Later, she knocked on the door as I sat on the bed in the guest room, scrolling through my phone. "It's just me," she said.

"Come on in," I called.

She opened the door a crack. "Just checking to make sure you've settled in okay."

"You always make me feel at home here. Your family is so great."

She pressed her lips together and looked at the floor like there was something else she wanted to say. "I know I agreed with you in the kitchen, but honestly, I think you should file a report with the police." She looked up at me, and her forehead creased. "Why do I feel like there's something you're not telling me?"

I shrugged. "I don't know." I looked her in the eyes so she wouldn't suspect I was lying.

Her face relaxed. "Well..." She drew her lips together. "If there is anything I can do at all ..." Her words trailed off.

"I'll let you know."

She gave a slow nod. "Right." She looked like she wanted to say more. "Good night," I said. I didn't want to lie to Davida, but I felt I had to protect her.

She pulled the door closed. The latch clicked, and I listened as she padded down the hallway to her room.

Later that night, something pulled me out of a deep, dreamless sleep. The wall greeted me, only inches from my nose. The guest room at Davida's was never completely dark. The porch light bled through the curtains, casting a blue glow around the room. I didn't have to turn around to know someone else was there with me. I felt his eyes on my back. I swallowed the lump in my throat, my heart hammering in my chest. I rolled over, holding my breath as if doing so would hold in my terror. Raoul stood in the corner. Shadows obscured his face, but I knew it was him. Being in his presence tapped into a primal fear deep inside me.

He stepped forward, allowing the blue glow of the light to fall upon his face. Even though I knew it was him before that moment, I gasped at the sight of him, the hollow of his cheeks, and the curve of his lips. Outwardly, he looked so normal, but I knew what lay beneath the surface. I'd seen what he really was. I sat up. My first instinct was to call out, but I knew no one within the sound of my voice could help me.

I opened my mouth to speak, but my voice caught in my throat. "What…" I held my hand up to my throat and cleared it. "Why are you doing this to me?" I had to squeeze the words out.

He stepped closer to the bed, his feet silent on the thick carpet.

I drew back, not wanting him to be too close to me. I was aware of the wall behind me.

He stood between me and the door. "I'm not doing anything to you. You're doing all of this to me." Sadness passed over his face. "Are you dreaming?"

The suggestion made me hope I was.

"Are you?" His dark eyes burrowed into me. He bent over so his face was level with mine.

I pressed myself against the wall behind me. Sweat gathered on my upper lip. I looked at the door over his shoulder, willing someone to walk by and open it, but the entire house was silent. I could picture everyone else in my mind sleeping soundly in their beds, having good dreams, and here I was, living a nightmare where the person I feared most in this world was in the room with me. I considered screaming, but I knew what I'd seen before. I knew what he could become if I upset him. So I sat with my heart hammering in my chest. He sat on my bed, the mattress sinking beneath his weight.

I scooted back even further, the smooth plaster of the wall against the bare skin of my arm. "I cannot force you to do anything," he said. The words slipped from his lips like oil.

A memory pricked my brain, but it didn't make sense. There were no images, only a feeling of loss and the smell of orange blossoms. What was that memory connected too? My mind was working far too fast to grasp it. "Why are you here? Why won't you leave me alone?"

The slightest smirk passed over his lips, and his weight shifted, moving the mattress. "Because you are mine, and I want you to remember."

Davida and her husband slept soundly in their bed. Their boys were being carried away by dreams in their own rooms. Why couldn't I be granted the same security? That was what I'd worked so hard for all these years. I thought I had found it. I thought safety and security was finally mine, but then this happened.

He reached out his hand to me, placing it on my arm. I flinched under the touch of his skin, cool and dry against my own. He looked into my eyes. "You can't stay here," he whispered.

His voice sent a chill through me, causing the hairs on the back of my neck to stand on end. I didn't try to pull my arm away. Instead, I stayed very still.

"You don't belong here." He leaned in so close that I could feel his hot breath on my face. "You belong with me."

I squeezed my eyes closed. I shouldn't have come here. I didn't want to expose Davida and her family to what he truly was.

"Why are you making this so difficult? I didn't want to do it this way. I thought that if you would only present yourself to me willingly, it could all end differently this time, but you always have to be so stubborn."

He removed his hand from my arm, and I wondered if escape was possible, but he was between me and the door. Any sound I would make would put people I love in danger. That was the last thing I wanted. I was trapped. The reality gripped me like a vice. I choked back a sob. My thoughts fogged. I couldn't think of anything, especially not how to escape. This was never who I wanted to be.

A moist, squelching sound rippled through the air. The sweet smell of rot bloomed around me. I didn't want to look. I couldn't witness the horror of his true face again. I only wanted to run.

"Khadijah." My name seeped from his lips.

I didn't look up at him. Instead, I looked down at the crumpled sheets in my lap. I fantasized about getting out of bed and running past him through the door, but I knew there would be no escaping him.

"Khadijah, look at me," he commanded.

Then I felt a warm, slick tentacle on my cheek, and I gasped, finding my voice for a moment. I let out a small yelp. My lips parted long enough for it to slip inside my mouth. First one and then another. They filled my mouth, forcing their way down my throat. I gagged, my flesh stretching painfully and my breath wheezing out of me until there was no air at all. My eyes opened wide, and I finally looked at him, my last attempt at getting help before it was too late.

The shape of him was different this time. He was still a monster, but I recognized him this time. It all made sense now.

"I'm sorry. I didn't want it to be this way." His voice was inside of my head. His thoughts melded with my own.

"Neither did I," I thought as I lost consciousness.

CHapTer 30

M emories flooded into me. I knew all of it. I remembered the first day he gave me that dress, the softness of cloth against my skin, and the joy and regret I felt as I twirled for him on unsure feet. The newness of it all was not enough to heal my wounded heart. He was right. We were meant to be together. That was our assignment. That was what the elders had told us.

"No matter where you go or what you do, you will always be mine. That is the way it is meant to be." He had grabbed hold of my arm, digging his fingers into the flesh. There was a time when I was naïve enough to think that ridding myself of this flesh suit was a guaranteed escape. I was wrong. When the elders want something to happen, it will happen no matter what. They made all of this sound like my choice, but it wasn't really. I have been running from this "choice" for years, disobeying the directive to take over this land and trying desperately to bury the memories of who I was. If it wasn't for Raoul, I would've been able to start over and forget everything in the past.

I could've built a good life here, but he wouldn't let me. He would prefer I was a slave to his intentions.

As the memories flowed back into me, I realized what this had been about all along. I had found my will, and he was still trying to take it from me.

"I didn't want to force it, but you made me." His words entered my mind and found their way into the crevices between my thoughts. "You make it all so hard. This could be easy for you. All you have to do is cooperate."

I gagged as his tentacles rammed down my throat, cutting off my air. They sucked at the tissue deep inside of me, pulling my flesh.

It was like he was flipping a switch inside me, turning on memories I couldn't access before. Suddenly, I remembered everyone I was in the past and who I was in the moment.

My skin split. The tearing started at the corners of my mouth, where he forced it open to make room for his probing tentacles. The flesh stretched thin. The bones of my jaw wrenched open until they cracked. What should have hurt did not because my body was not my own. I was separate from it in a way I had known all along but hadn't been able to access. My face opened to reveal who I really was. I let the part of me that had been locked away unfurl. The freedom of it was exhilarating.

He was stronger than me, but I was more determined. I had proven that every time I had blown up my assigned life and decided to move on. And I would do it again. I would move on without him because I would not allow them to tell me what I could and could not do or who I could and could not be.

"I am not yours. I am no one's." I pushed him away, expelling his thick tentacles from me. Each woman who had taken her own life in order to escape him was me. I had chosen to start over again and again because I knew I was more than this role my elders had tried to slot me into. I could no longer be happy in this flesh suit. It was time to leave and remember everything. My skin bubbled and split, opening me to the truth of who I was.

Timeless.

Endless.

Powerful beyond measure.

And no one, not even a monster, could hold me back because, underneath it all, I was the monster all along. Once I decided to stop running, I realized that there was nothing to run from.

NOTE FROM THE AUTHOR

T hank you for reading The Curse of Warner Manor. This is the first book in a series called The Farrington Phenomenon. It's a series about the strange goings-on in a small upstate New York town. The town is completely fictional. I usually write about Florida because that's where I live now, but I grew up in the northeast and wanted to set a few books there. It's fun to have a change of scenery.

If you pay attention, you'll notice some characters from the Suncoast Paranormal series make appearances in upcoming books in The Farrington Phenomenon. I like to put little or not-so-little Easter eggs in my books. They all exist in the same universe, and characters from other series will make cameos in various books. In the next book in the series, you'll find out that someone in The Curse of Warner Manor is related to someone from one of the Suncoast Paranormal books. I have fun tying the books together like that. I hope it's fun for you too.

I appreciate your support. Ever since I was a little girl all I ever wanted to do was be a writer. I'm so happy to share the stories I write with you. If you want to learn a little more about my writing, be the first to find out about new books, and learn about some fun spooky things, sign up for my newsletter. Just go to my website, LovelynBet tison.com.

ABOUT THE AUTHOR

Lovelyn Bettison lives in Florida with her husband, son, and elderly dog. When she's not writing, she's reading a much-anticipated library book or watching horror movies. She also likes playing eighties pop songs on her mountain dulcimer, tending to her permaculture garden, and hanging out in local coffee shops. She's so happy to have the chance to share her stories with people like you. Find out more about her and her books at lovelynbettison.com

www.ingramcontent.com/pod-product-compliance
Lightning Source LLC
Chambersburg PA
CBHW031230260626
47169CB00007B/2235